The Professor's Brat

ROSE GOLD

The Professor's Brat Series

Book One

By T. W. Sams

The Professor's Brat: Rose Gold

The Professor's Brat Series, Book One

Copyright © 2025 by T. W. Sams

Dedication

For M,

Your inspiration lit the first spark, and your patient ears carried this story to life.

Thank you for listening, for encouraging, and for being the heart behind the heat.

With gratitude,

T.W.

TABLE OF CONTENTS

Sienna Holloway

S ienna's ponytail whipped behind her as she hurried across the bustling Redwood Springs Community College campus, crimson hair flashing like a flare among the sea of students. She clutched her books tightly to her chest, as if they could shield her from the chaos and noise pressing in from all sides. Her gaze remained lowered as she wove through the jostling bodies, avoiding eye contact.

The peeling paint of the main building loomed ahead, a shabby refuge. Sienna slipped inside the tattered hallway where yellowed linoleum and mustiness spoke of age and neglect. Faded posters curled on corkboards lining the corridor.

Her eyes darted as she absorbed the surroundings, taking in small details—the ancient payphone hanging crookedly on the wall, the notices for campus clubs, a flier for used textbooks. The college felt like another world from the strict Christian high school of her youth.

Students filed past her into classrooms, a few curious glances sliding over the petite redhead frozen in shock by the doorway. Sienna shrank back, pulse fluttering. She swallowed hard. "Okay," she told herself timidly, clamping down on the urge to flee back to the safety and solitude of her bedroom.

Straightening her spine, she gripped the printed schedule in her damp palm and scanned the classroom numbers, searching for Introductory World History. Her stomach clenched with a mix of anxiety and anticipation. The first step in her new life.

She slid into a seat near the back of the classroom, hoping to remain inconspicuous. The room buzzed with chatter as students filed in, their voices blending into an indistinguishable hum. She kept her eyes down, focusing on the scratched surface of the wooden desk, tracing the lines and initials carved by generations of bored students.

At twenty-six, she was a late bloomer in the academic world, her conservative upbringing having delayed her pursuit of higher education. The years she'd spent working menial jobs and living under her parents' restrictive rules had only intensified her hunger for knowledge and independence.

A tall, distinguished-looking man with salt-and-pepper hair and a neatly trimmed beard stepped inside. He carried himself with an air of quiet authority, his presence immediately commanding the room's attention.

The student in front of her grumbled, shifting uncomfortably as Professor Hayes entered the room. Known for his high expectations and tough love approach, he quickly assessed the students with a sharp gaze. Even the most confident students were intimidated by his presence.

Sienna was speechless as she observed the newcomer's appearance. Her breath seemed to freeze in her throat. Professor Hayes exuded an aura of confidence and intellect that both intimidated and intrigued her. His dark eyes scanned the room, seeming to take in every face in an instant.

As he spoke about his background and his approach to teaching, Sienna found herself hanging on his every word. There was something magnetic about him, a charisma that drew her in despite her usual shyness.

The Professor's resonant voice filled the classroom. Sienna found her anxiety slowly ebbing away, replaced by a growing fascination with the subject matter. History had always intrigued her, but hearing it discussed with such passion and depth was electrifying. She leaned forward in her seat, drinking in every word, her pen flying across the page as she took meticulous notes.

The cycle of lectures and classes continued through the day, each one bleeding into the next until they were indistinguishable. But Professor Hayes' class stood out like a vivid brushstroke against a muted background.

Her first round of classes came to an end, and she found herself drawn to the library, a modern building that stood apart from the weathered structures of the main campus. She pushed through the heavy doors, the hushed atmosphere enveloping her like a soothing balm.

The scent of books and the soft whisper of turning pages beckoned her deeper into the library's embrace. Sienna wandered through the stacks, trailing her fingers along the spines of countless volumes, each one holding the promise of knowledge and escape.

In a secluded corner, far from the main entrance, she discovered a small study area bathed in the warm glow of a lamp. The plush armchair invited her to sink into its depths, to lose herself in the pages of a book and forget the overwhelming reality of her new life.

With a gentle sigh, she settled into the chair and pulled her well-worn history textbook from her faded canvas bag. The spine was cracked, and the pages were starting to yellow with age. It was listed as "usable," and was all she could afford from the limited options at the campus bookstore.

The lighting of the library cast shadows across her face, accentuating the gentle curve of her cheekbones and the intensity of her concentration. Her red hair, pulled back in a practical ponytail, was now beginning to fall in soft waves around her shoulders, a subtle rebellion against the constraints of her conservative upbringing.

The text seemed to come alive under her fingertips, each word a whisper of the past, drawing her deeper into the complex web of historical events. Sienna's mind raced, absorbing the information with a quiet passion, her desire to impress her instructor fueling her determination. The weight of the centuries seemed to press down on her, the distant voices of long-gone eras echoing in her mind.

The sound of footsteps intruded upon her solitude. She glanced up, her eyes wide and wary, as a group of classmates passed by her table. Their gazes flickered over her, a mixture of curiosity and confusion evident in their expressions. Sienna felt the familiar pang of social awkwardness, the sense of being an outsider in a world she couldn't quite understand.

She lowered her eyes, her fingers tightening around the edges of the textbook, as if it were a lifeline in a sea of uncertainty. The weight of their stares pressed down upon her with discomfort. Sienna wished she could disappear, to melt into the shadows and become one with the books that surrounded her.

As footsteps faded into the distance, Sienna released a shaky breath, her shoulders sagging with a mixture of relief and exhaustion. She turned back to her textbook, her fingers caressing the worn pages with a reverence born of desperation and determination. She lost herself once more in the comforting embrace of knowledge, her heart aching for a connection she feared she might never find.

A soft voice broke through her concentration, startling her from the depths of her studies. She looked up, her heart racing as she met the curious gaze of a fellow student. He stood before her, a friendly smile on his lips, his eyes glinting with a warmth that seemed to penetrate the very walls she had so carefully constructed around herself.

"Hey there," he said, his voice rich and inviting. "Mind if I join you?"

Sienna's mouth went dry, her tongue heavy and unwieldy in her mouth. She wanted to respond, to welcome the opportunity for companionship, but the words seemed like a foreign language in her throat. Her gaze darted back to the safety of her textbook, the pages blurring before her eyes as she struggled to find her voice.

"I ... I'm just studying," she stammered, her cheeks burning with embarrassment. "I don't want to bother you."

The young man chuckled. "You're not bothering me. I saw your history textbook and was hoping we could study together. I sat in front of you in class this morning. Professor Hayes can be pretty overwhelming. This is my second time taking that class."

Sienna's heart leapt at the prospect, a flicker of hope igniting within her chest. But even as she yearned to accept his offer, the fear that had become her constant companion reared its ugly head, whispering doubts and insecurities in her ear.

What if she said something stupid? What if he realized just how awkward and out of place she truly was? The thought of rejection, of once again being cast aside and left alone, was almost too much to bear.

"I ... I'm sorry," she whispered, her voice trembling as she forced the words past the lump in her throat. "I don't think so."

She could feel the weight of the stranger's gaze upon her. His curiosity was evident even though he said nothing. Sienna wished she could sink into the floor, to escape this moment and return to the safe solitude of her studies.

"Sorry," he said with a shrug, breaking the silence that had stretched on for what felt like an eternity. "I didn't mean to bug you."

There was something about him that made her want to trust him, but years of disappointment and loneliness held her back. She had learned long ago that people were fickle creatures, prone to turning their backs when things got tough.

With that, she buried her nose back into her book, her eyes stinging with unshed tears as she heard the young man's footsteps retreating into the distance.

The library's hushed atmosphere began to shift. Students, one by one, started to pack up their belongings, the soft rustling of papers and the muted zipping of backpacks filling the air. The end of the day had arrived, and with it, the inevitable dispersal of the crowd.

Sienna stood and gathered her things. She walked through the empty corridors of Redwood Springs, her footsteps echoing on the linoleum floor. The setting sun cast an eerie orange glow through the windows as she clutched her books tightly and lost herself in thought while navigating the deserted campus.

Donovan Hayes

The timeworn walls of the history classroom stood silent witness to Professor Donovan Hayes' oratory dance through time. The air itself seemed to thicken with anticipation, each word from his lips not merely spoken, but conjured, painting epochs and empires with a dark, velvety cadence that demanded attention.

"History is not just a chronicle of dates and events," Hayes declared, his baritone voice wrapping around the students like a shroud. "It is the very essence of our collective soul, a tapestry woven with the threads of human ambition, folly, and desire."

The room was charged, energy pulsing from Donovan at the front to eager minds in the back. He was an anchor guiding them through the fog of ages past, while pens scratched against paper in the enraptured audience.

"Consider the rise and fall of civilizations," he intoned. "The ebb and flow of power—how it shapes not only the contours of our world but the very core of our being."

In the dim light of the aging classroom, Hayes' silhouette appeared both part of the present and yet somehow removed—a specter of knowledge that transcended the here and now. His words wove a spellbinding narrative, a siren song that pulled his students steadily into the depths of contemplation and wonder.

Amidst this pageant of rapt attention, a singular presence stood out: Sienna Holloway, her striking red hair a vivid flame against the drab backdrop of peeling paint and worn desks. A quick turn of her head caused her hair to reflect the morning sun, drawing Donovan's gaze for an imperceptible moment. The connection was fleeting, yet it lingered like the afterglow of a comet's trail.

In that charged atmosphere, where the air itself seemed thick with the dust of ancient tomes and the spirit of inquiry, the world outside faded until there was nothing but the deep timbre of Donovan's voice, the compendium of history laid bare, and the silent, simmering connection that danced like shadows between lecturer and pupil.

Sienna's gaze lingered on Donovan, her breath catching in the wake of his every syllable. His voice stretched across the room, touching her in ways that left her skin tingling with an awareness she didn't dare name. The rumble of his voice found its way through the maze of desks, wrapping around her like a velvet shroud, and in those moments, it felt as though he spoke only to her. She leaned forward, her elbows resting on the scratched surface of her desk, emerald eyes wide not just with scholarly intent but with a burgeoning fascination that sank deep into her bones.

The contrast between them was stark. Sienna, with her modest attire and the gentle coil of her red hair restrained in a functional ponytail, exuded an air of unassuming simplicity. Her presence small against the backdrop of Donovan's command—a quiet, unobtrusive spirit so often overlooked in the bustle of academia. Yet here, under the spell of his lecture, her shyness did not feel like a cloak to hide beneath, but rather a vantage point from which to observe the force before her.

Donovan dominated the podium, his towering figure imposing and commanding. His crisply ironed shirt clung to chiseled muscles, a facade of professionalism that contrasted with the intensity in his eyes and movements. Each deliberate motion, each calculated pause, hinted at a hidden depth beneath his tough exterior. Sienna was captivated by this puzzle of a man, eager to unravel the layers and reveal the true story behind his captivating presence.

A mysterious smile would occasionally dance upon his lips, offering fleeting glimpses into a world beyond the walls of the classroom. Sienna's heart thrummed with a strange rhythm, her academic curiosity entwining with a more primal interest. The contrasts of her timidity against his assertive eloquence created a tension that hummed through her, electric and alive.

For Sienna, Donovan's eyes seemed to gaze beyond the immediacy of the classroom, as though he peered directly into the essence of bygone eras. When class was released, piercing the hypnotic spell, there was a collective exhale, as if the room itself had been holding its breath, reluctant to release the enigma that was Donovan Hayes.

She couldn't shake the magnetic pull of Donovan's presence. It was as if he held all the answers to life's mysteries, and she wanted nothing more than to unravel them with him. But at the same time, she was hesitant. Unsure of whether acting on her attraction to him was a good idea. She debated sitting near him tomorrow, torn between her desire to be closer to him and her fear of the potential consequences.

Growing Attraction

Her usual corner in the back called to her like a siren song of safety, but Sienna steeled her nerves and forced herself forward. The click of her sensible flats echoed loudly in the quiet room as she made her way through the door, sliding into an empty seat in the second row.

As she pulled out her notebook with shaking hands, the door swung open. Professor Hayes entered, his presence immediately filling the room. Sienna watched him stride purposefully to the podium. His dark sweater stretched across broad shoulders, hinting at the strength beneath.

He began his lecture, and Sienna was in awe. She had always been a diligent student, but she had never been so captivated by a teacher before. His voice was deep and smooth, each word rolling off his tongue with precision and purpose. His dark eyes rested on Sienna. Their gaze met for a few moments before he looked away.

"What am I doing here?" She thought, her cheeks flushing. This was madness. She should be safe in her corner, not exposing herself like this. But even as doubt crept in, Sienna knew she couldn't go back now. Something indefinable but irresistible pulled her towards him. All she could do was hold on tight and see where it led her.

As he cleared his throat to begin, Sienna unconsciously leaned forward in her seat.

"Today, we delve into the intricacies of the Industrial Revolution," Professor Hayes began, his deep voice rumbling through the hall like distant thunder.

Sienna felt the vibrations of his words in her chest. She fumbled for her pen, desperate to capture every word, yet finding it increasingly difficult to focus on anything but the mesmerizing cadence of his voice.

His hands moved with graceful authority as he gestured, emphasizing key points. "Consider the societal upheaval," he continued, pacing slowly in front of the podium. "The shift from agrarian to urban life..."

"I shouldn't be here," Sienna thought, her heart racing. "This close, it's too much." But she couldn't look away, couldn't stop her senses from drinking in every aspect of him. The way his shirt pulled taut across his shoulders as he wrote on the board. The faint scent of his cologne, barely detectable but utterly intoxicating.

With each passing moment, Sienna felt herself being drawn deeper into Professor Hayes' world, a world of knowledge and power that both frightened and thrilled her. She gripped her pen tighter, anchoring herself to reality as her mind swam with possibilities she'd never dared contemplate before.

Suddenly, Professor Hayes turned. For a fleeting moment, his eyes locked with Sienna's. She wanted to look away, to break the intensity of the connection, but found herself unable to do so.

Professor Hayes' lips quirked in the faintest hint of a smile before he continued his lecture, leaving Sienna reeling. She sucked in a shaky breath, her cheeks flushing with warmth that seemed to spread throughout her entire body.

As the lecture reached its crescendo, Professor Hayes' voice grew more impassioned. "The very fabric of society was rewoven," he declared, his words weaving a tapestry of history that enveloped the room.

A wave of conflicting emotions crashed over her, causing panic and excitement to battle for dominance within her. She frantically crossed her legs, attempting to suppress the growing tension that seemed to course through her veins, making her skin feel too sensitive.

She watched as Hayes shuffled papers, his long fingers moving deftly and leaving Sienna mesmerized. She imagined those hands ... No. She shook her head, trying to dispel the inappropriate thoughts.

The clock ticked closer to dismissal and the shifting students around her shattered the spell that held Sienna captive. Chairs scraped against the floor, bags rustled, and voices filled the air, but Sienna remained rooted to her seat.

Her heart raced as the classroom emptied. She knew she should leave, but something kept her tethered to her seat. Her eyes darted between the exit and the imposing figure at the podium, indecision paralyzing her.

"What am I doing?" She thought, her palms damp with nervous sweat. "This is ridiculous. I should just go."

But she couldn't. The pull was too strong, the desire to be near him, to hear his voice again.

Sienna gathered her belongings. She stood on shaky legs, her breath coming in short, quick gasps. The distance between her seat and the podium seemed insurmountable, a chasm she wasn't sure she had the courage to cross.

Step by hesitant step, Sienna approached Professor Hayes. The sound of her heartbeat drowned out everything else. She clutched her notebook to her chest like a shield, her knuckles white with tension.

She swallowed hard. "P-Professor Hayes?" she stammered, her voice barely audible, even to her own ears.

Donovan turned, his piercing gaze locking onto her. "Yes, Miss...?" His deep voice rumbled through her, setting her nerves alight.

"H-Holloway," Sienna stuttered as she timidly introduced herself. "Sienna Holloway."

"What can I do for you, Ms. Holloway?"

Her heart raced as she licked her lips, struggling to form coherent words. She nervously settled into the chair directly in front of him, unable to muster the courage to stand. "I was wondering about Cleopatra's influence on Roman politics," she finally stammered out.

A flush of embarrassment flooded her cheeks as she posed her question. The topic of study was the Industrial Revolution, yet here she was, breaking the flow with a question about ancient Roman politics.

Hayes' eyebrow arched slightly, a flicker of interest crossing his features. "An intriguing observation," he replied, his tone clipped yet somehow inviting.

Despite trying to maintain a professional demeanor, he stole several glances down her loose blouse. A faint flush rose on his cheeks, betraying his internal struggle between professionalism and desire. He could just make out the gentle curves of her body and tried his best to remain composed, but his eyes gave him away.

"She had exceptional political skills; however Cleopatra is most remembered for her beauty. Her strategic alliances with both Caesar and Mark Antony were proof of her diplomatic abilities and manipulative tactics."

Sienna found herself drawn in, mesmerized by the passion underlying his words. Her fear melted away, replaced by a burning curiosity—not just about history, but about the man before her.

Other questions entered her mind. Was it intentional, the way she leaned in and showed just enough cleavage to catch Professor Hayes' attention? Did he think less of her now? Or worse, did she embarrass herself?

Or was Donovan excited by the glimpses he caught? A hot sensation ignited in her thighs as she recalled the way Professor Hayes' eyes glanced at her young breasts. Was he truly drawn to her question, or did he covet more than being an influence on her education?

She subtly tugged on her blouse, allowing a little more of her supple cleavage to show, causing an undeniable grin to spread across Donovan's face.

Suspicions confirmed.

Her senses were overwhelmed by Professor Hayes. His cologne, a heady mixture of sandalwood and something uniquely masculine, wafted towards her with each of his movements. The scent was intoxicating, making her head swim and her pulse quicken.

The click of the wall clock echoed through the room, signaling the impending start of the next class. Sienna reluctantly began to stand up, her movements slow and deliberate, while Donovan began greeting the incoming students.

Her mind whirled with questions. Who was this man, really? What secrets lay behind those piercing eyes? The urge to follow him, to learn more, was almost overwhelming.

She hugged her textbook to her chest, trying to ground herself. "Get it together, Sienna," she chided internally. Yet even as she admonished herself, she knew it was futile. The seed of fascination had been planted and it would not be easily uprooted.

The lingering scent of his cologne seemed to mock her, a ghostly reminder of his presence. Sienna closed her eyes, inhaling deeply, committing the aroma to memory. When she opened them again, determination had replaced uncertainty in her gaze.

"Holy shit," she silently whispered to herself. "He's delicious."

A Plan

Sienna's fingers hovered over the keyboard, her heart racing as she typed "Donovan Hayes" into the search bar for the thousandth time. The soft glow of her laptop screen illuminated her face in the dimness of her cramped bedroom, casting shadows that accentuated the dark circles under her eyes. She hadn't slept properly in days, her mind consumed by thoughts of her bewildering professor.

As the search results populated, Sienna leaned in closer, her eyes scanning frantically for any new information. She clicked through familiar academic profiles and dry faculty pages, desperation growing with each fruitless link. Her fingers trembled slightly as she scrolled, the quiet tapping of the mouse the only sound in the stillness of the night.

"There has to be more," she whispered to herself. "What are you hiding, Professor Hayes?"

Sienna's gaze flickered to the clock on her nightstand—1:27 am. She should sleep, but the allure of uncovering Donovan's secrets was too strong. With a sigh, she returned to her search, clicking on a link she hadn't noticed before.

There, in crisp black and white, was a conference schedule for the upcoming Historical Association meeting. Listed among the guest speakers was none other than Professor Donovan Hayes.

"There you are," Sienna breathed, her heart pounding loudly. She leaned back in her chair, running her hands through her tangled red hair, her mind racing with possibilities.

The conference was in just two weeks. Two weeks until she could see him in a setting far removed from the stuffy confines of the classroom. Sienna's imagination ran wild, conjuring images of Donovan commanding a room with his authoritative voice, his presence magnetic and irresistible.

She bit her lip, a familiar warmth spreading through her body as she pictured herself in the audience, hanging on to his every word. Would he notice her? Would their eyes meet across the crowded room? She shook her head, trying to clear the fantasy from her mind. "Get a grip," she muttered to herself, but she couldn't stop the smile that spread across her face. This was her chance—to see him, to learn more about him, to maybe even...

No. She wouldn't let herself finish that thought. Instead, she turned back to her laptop, determination set in her jaw as she began to research the conference in earnest. She had two weeks to prepare, and she wasn't going to waste a single moment.

She delved deeper into the conference details. Her eyes widened as she discovered the venue - the prestigious Belmont Hotel. The name alone evoked images of luxury and sophistication, a far cry from the shabby community college where she usually encountered Donovan.

Her fingers trembled as she dialed the hotel's number, her heart racing with anticipation.

"Belmont Hotel, how may I assist you?" a cheerful voice answered.

"Hi, I'm calling to confirm a reservation for the Historical Association Conference," Sienna said softly. She paused, then added with feigned nonchalance, "It's for Professor Donovan Hayes. Which room will he be in? I'm his ... assistant. I'll need to deliver some materials to him."

The lie tasted bitter on her tongue, but the thrill of potential success overrode her discomfort.

"Let me check on that for you, ma'am," the receptionist replied. Sienna held her breath, listening to the faint tapping of keys. "It looks like Professor Hayes is assigned to room 412."

Sienna's pulse quickened. "I am hoping you can help me book a room rather close to his."

Her fingers tightened around the phone as she struggled to keep her voice steady.

"Something on the same floor would be ideal."

There was a brief pause as the receptionist checked availability. "We have room 408 open. It's just two doors up from Professor Hayes. Would that suit your needs?"

"Perfect," Sienna breathed, trying to hide her giddiness. "I'll take it."

As she finished the booking process, she felt a mix of exhilaration and guilt wash over her. This was crossing a line. But the thought of being so close to Donovan, of potentially running into him in the hallway or catching a glimpse of him entering or leaving his room, was intoxicating.

Sienna hung up and collapsed back onto her bed, her heart pounding. She closed her eyes, imagining the scenario playing out. Would she have the courage to approach him outside of the conference setting? What would she say? How would he react to seeing her there?

She allowed herself to indulge in the fantasy of accidentally bumping into Donovan in the hotel hallway, of feeling the electricity between them as they exchanged pleasantries.

"This is crazy," she whispered to herself, but the smile on her face persisted. For once in her life, Sienna Holloway was taking a risk, stepping out of her carefully protected world and into something thrilling and unknown.

She closed her eyes, picturing Donovan's face, imagining the timbre of his voice as he delivered his keynote address. "Soon," she whispered to herself, a promise and a prayer intertwined.

As the days ticked by, she found herself obsessing over everything from what she would wear to how she would act if they happened to cross paths.

She had already packed several outfits for the duration of the conference, but now she was second-guessing everything. Did she have enough professional attire? What if she ran into Donovan outside of the conference and wasn't dressed just right?

Finally, the day arrived.

She moved through her morning routine in a daze. She showered quickly, the hot water doing little to calm her nerves. As she toweled off, she caught sight of herself in the steamy mirror—cheeks flushed, eyes bright with anticipation. She barely recognized the woman staring back at her.

Sienna dressed casually in dark jeans and a soft sweater, comfortable for the long drive ahead but nice enough in case she ran into her Professor at the hotel. She applied a touch of makeup, her hands shaking slightly as she swiped on mascara. "Get it together," she muttered to herself, taking another steadying breath.

She hefted her overstuffed suitcase down the narrow staircase of her childhood home; the wheels clattering loudly in the early morning quiet. Her beat-up hatchback awaited her outside. She opened the hatch and grunted as she lifted her heavy suitcase inside. She had packed far too much, but the thought of being unprepared to see Donovan in any possible scenario had driven her to excess.

Her hands gripped the steering wheel tightly. She took a deep breath, inhaling the familiar scent of old leather and the pine air freshener hanging from her rearview mirror. She turned the key in the ignition, and the car sputtered to life.

The first rays of dawn were just beginning to streak across the sky, painting the world in soft hues of pink and gold. The streets of her sleepy hometown were deserted, the silence broken only by the low rumble of her car's engine.

The drive stretched before her, a ribbon of asphalt cutting through the changing landscape. As she left the familiar confines of her town behind, she felt a mixture of exhilaration and terror coursing through her veins. She was really doing this—driving to a conference where she had no business being, all for the chance to catch a glimpse of Donovan outside the classroom.

The miles ticked by, marked by the steady rhythm of her windshield wipers as they battled against a light drizzle. Finally pulling in the valet line, she stepped out of her car, her eyes widening as she took in the grandeur of the Belmont Hotel. Its gleaming glass façade stretched skyward, reflecting the afternoon sun. A doorman in an impeccably pressed uniform rushed forward to assist her with her luggage.

"Welcome to the Belmont, miss," he said with a polite nod.

Sienna mustered up a timid smile. "Thank you," her voice muted against the noise of the bustling city street. She hesitantly handed her keys to the valet, a service she had never experienced before. She gave him a twenty-dollar bill as a tip, to which he happily responded by giving her a valet ticket and explaining how to retrieve her car anytime she needed it. She nodded along with his instructions, but the excitement coursing through her body made it difficult for her to fully comprehend what was being said.

The lobby's opulence nearly took her breath away. Marble floors and plush velvet sofas were illuminated by the warm radiance of crystal chandeliers.

The air was perfumed with the subtle scent of jasmine. Soft classical music drifted from hidden speakers.

"It's beautiful," Sienna breathed, her gaze darting around the space. She wondered if Professor Hayes was already here, perhaps sitting in one of those elegant armchairs or enjoying a drink at the gleaming bar.

A smartly dressed woman greeted her at the front desk. "Checking in?"

Sienna nodded, her throat suddenly dry. "Yes, room 408, please."

Sienna's mind wandered as the receptionist processed her check-in. What if Donovan was in his room right now? What if their paths crossed in the elevator? The possibilities made her pulse quicken.

"Here's your key card, Ms. Holloway. Enjoy your stay."

Sienna clutched the card, feeling as though she'd been handed a key to a secret world. "Thank you," she managed.

She made her way to the elevators. The doors slid open with a soft chime, and she stepped inside, her finger hovering over the button for the fourth floor.

This is it, she thought. There's no turning back now.

As the elevator doors opened on the fourth floor, Sienna stepped out into a quiet corridor, lined with standard hotel carpet. Her heart raced as she scanned the area for room 408. With each step, she glanced back, torn between anticipation and fear of seeing Professor Hayes behind her.

She found her room and fumbled with the key card. The lock beeped, and she pushed the door open, stepping into a space that smelled of crisp linens and subtle floral notes.

She set her bag down and sank onto the edge of the king-sized bed, her fingers tracing the smooth comforter. She closed her eyes, taking a deep breath to steady herself.

"What am I doing?" she whispered to the empty room. The enormity of her actions crashed over her like a wave. She was here, two doors from Professor Hayes, the man who occupied her thoughts day and night.

She stood, smoothing her sweater. "I need to explore."

She left her room and made her way back to the elevator. As the doors opened, she nearly collided with a tall figure stepping out.

"Oh, I'm so sorry—" Sienna began, eyes locked on the floor, then froze as she slowly lifted her head, recognizing the commanding presence of Professor Donovan Hayes.

His dark eyes met hers. "Ms. Holloway, is it?" his deep voice resonated in her spine. "What a pleasant surprise."

"H-Hi, Professor."

Her voice came out in a squeak. She felt his eyes on her as she stepped into the elevator, his familiar cologne triggering a flood of anxious thoughts in her mind as the doors closed.

Her heart raced as she stepped into the lobby, her eyes drawn to a large display board near the banquet hall entrance. She scanned the schedule until her gaze locked onto that familiar name: "Professor Donovan Hayes—The Child Emperors of Rome: Power and Vulnerability in Ancient Politics."

A flutter of excitement bloomed in her chest. "Tomorrow at 2 pm," she whispered, her fingers ghosting over the printed words.

As the evening approached, Sienna's stomach twisted with a mix of hunger and nerves. She smoothed her hair and made her way to the hotel restaurant.

"Table for one, please," she said softly to the hostess, who led her to a small table near the center of the room.

Sienna sat on the edge of her chair, nervously scanning the dimly lit room. The elegant space was illuminated by crystal chandeliers, casting a soft glow over the pristine white tablecloths and gleaming silverware.

"Can I get you started with a drink?" A waiter appeared, startling her.

"Oh, um, just water, please."

She wondered whether Professor Hayes would be dining in the same restaurant. The mere thought made her palms damp.

"Get a grip," she chided herself internally. "You're just here to watch."

But even as she tried to calm herself, her eyes continued to scan the room, searching for that commanding presence that had captivated her so completely.

Her senses heightened to a near-painful acuity. Every clink of cutlery, every deep laugh, every flash of movement drew her attention. Her fingers fidgeted with the stem of her water glass as she discreetly observed the other diners, searching for that familiar silhouette.

A group of academics at a nearby table caught her ear, making her wonder if they were conference attendees. She leaned in slightly, straining to catch a glimpse of their faces, hoping to see the sharp, intelligent features of Professor Hayes among them.

Suddenly, a rich, dark voice cut through the ambient noise of the restaurant.

She knew his voice.

She turned her head slowly, careful not to draw attention to herself.

There he was.

Professor Donovan Hayes stood near the bar, engaged in conversation with a silver-haired woman. Even in this casual setting, he exuded an air of authority. His lean frame was clothed in a crisp button-down shirt, the sleeves rolled up to reveal strong forearms. A pair of well-fitted dark jeans and polished loafers completed his look— professional, yet approachable.

Sienna's mouth went dry as she watched him. His strong jawline moved as he spoke, a smile on his lips. One hand held a tumbler of amber liquid, while the other gestured gracefully as he made a point.

"Oh God," Sienna thought, her cheeks flushing. "He's so HOT!"

She couldn't tear her eyes away, drinking in every detail. The way his brow furrowed slightly as he listened intently to his companion. The subtle flex of his fingers around his glass. The commanding way he held himself, shoulders back, spine straight.

A waiter appeared at her table, startling her. "Are you ready to order, miss?"

Sienna blinked, realizing she hadn't even glanced at the menu. "I ... I need a few more minutes, please," her eyes darting back to where Professor Hayes stood.

As the waiter walked away, Sienna's heart nearly stopped. Hayes was looking directly at her, his intense gaze meeting hers across the room as he raised his glass slightly in her direction before turning back to his conversation.

Her pulse raced, a mixture of excitement and trepidation flooding her veins.

She stared at the menu, trying to get her mind back to reality. Her hands trembled slightly as she scanned the options, the words blurring together. She settled on a Caesar salad, something simple and easy to digest. She was a nervous wreck, her stomach in knots.

When the waiter returned, she placed her order in a quiet, shaky voice, her eyes darting back to where Professor Hayes stood. He was still engaged in conversation, but she could have sworn his gaze flickered towards her once more.

Her salad arrived rather quickly, the familiar dressing a stark contrast to the turmoil in her mind. She picked at it absently, her appetite diminished by the nervous energy coursing through her. Her gaze kept drifting back to Professor Hayes.

As if he could read her thoughts, Hayes turned in his seat and locked eyes with her once again. This time, their gaze lingered for a just a moment. Sienna felt rooted to her spot, unable to break eye contact.

He flashed a smile at his companion, signaling the end of their meeting as he stood up from his chair, his forearms looking like dessert. Sienna's gaze remained fixed on him, not wanting to let go. He caught her eye again and chuckled at her obvious adoration.

With a few strides, he reached her table and gently rested a hand on her shoulder.

"I took care of your salad. Have a good evening, Ms. Holloway."

Sienna's mouth fell open in shock.

Her heart raced as she watched him walk away, unsure of whether to follow or let him go. What was he planning? Was this a test of their dynamic? A hidden message? Her mind was a jumbled mess of doubts and fears. She couldn't think straight, let alone make a decision about what to do next. Should she take a risk and chase after him or play it safe and stay put? The weight of uncertainty pressed down on her, paralyzing her in indecision.

She decided not to make a fool of herself and chose to retire to her room for the night. Her mind raced with thoughts of Professor Hayes. The weight of his gaze, the subtle curve of his lips as he raised his glass to her, paying for the overpriced salad—it all felt so surreal.

Inside her room, she leaned against the closed door, resting her eyes and taking a deep breath. The scent of his cologne seemed to linger in her nostrils. She couldn't shake the feeling that he was playing with her, testing her resolve.

The Conference

The sun slowly crept above the horizon and woke Sienna from her restless sleep. Unable to calm her anxious mind, she spent the morning pacing around the hotel grounds, lost in thoughts of the professor's upcoming presentation.

The clock struck noon with little fanfare, and lunch was nothing more than a bland turkey sandwich from the hotel lobby. The prepackaged meal did not satisfy her hunger, but it didn't matter—her mind was consumed with anticipation and nervousness about seeing Professor Hayes.

She stood in front of her overflowing luggage, feeling frustrated and indecisive. Each outfit she had packed for the weekend seemed to reflect a different aspect of her personality—some too youthful, others too polished. She couldn't figure out which version of herself she wanted to present. But with time quickly passing by, she knew she had to make a decision.

She dressed herself in a simple blouse and jeans. Was she overdressed? Underdressed? She couldn't decide on any of the options she packed. "It's too late to change now," she muttered to herself. With a deep breath, she headed out the door.

The entrance to the grand banquet hall loomed ahead with the sound of lively chatter greeting her. Uncertain of where to go or what to do, she stepped into the room and let herself wander aimlessly among the well-dressed professionals. She felt like a fish out of water, her discomfort and unease evident to those around her. She tried to blend in, but it was clear that she did not belong in this setting.

The hall buzzed with anticipation as Professor Hayes took the podium. Sienna sat near the back; her hands clasped tightly in her lap to keep them from fidgeting. She watched, entranced, as he adjusted the microphone and cleared his throat.

"Good afternoon, colleagues," he began, his deep voice resonating through the space. "Today, we'll be exploring the fascinating world of Rome's child emperors."

As he delved into the intricacies of ancient Roman politics, she found herself captivated not just by the content, but by his delivery. His hands moved expressively, emphasizing key points. His eyes sparkled with enthusiasm, occasionally sweeping across the audience.

"Did you know," he said, pausing for effect, "that Gordian III became emperor at the tender age of thirteen?"

Sienna leaned forward, biting her lip in sensual admiration. She jolted back, hoping no one had noticed her Freudian slip. She watched as her professor orated facts and quips to a captive audience.

Her mind drifted to places it shouldn't, imagining stolen moments with him and longing for a connection beyond the boundaries of their professional relationship.

She imagined his strong hands cupping her face, his deep voice whispering her name. The fantasy was so vivid that she nearly gasped aloud, catching herself just in time. She glanced around nervously, worried that someone might have noticed her flushed cheeks and quickened breath.

To her relief, the rest of the audience remained engrossed in the presentation, hanging on every word. Sienna forced herself to focus, trying to absorb the wealth of information being shared. Yet her eyes kept drifting back to his lips, watching them form each word with precision.

Applause filled the room, jolting Sienna back to Donovan's presentation reaching its conclusion. Her clapping was noticeably more vigorous than those around her. Flushing, she glanced around nervously, but most attendees were already rising from their seats, engaged in discussion.

Professor Hayes stepped down from the podium, immediately surrounded by colleagues. Sienna's heart raced. Should she approach him? Tell him how much she enjoyed the presentation?

"No," she thought, forcing herself to remain seated. "I can't. Not yet."

She watched longingly as he shook hands and fielded questions, fighting the urge to join the throng. Her fingers itched to reach out, to touch his arm, to feel the warmth of his skin beneath her fingertips.

"Get a grip, Sienna," she chided herself. "Chill out."

With a deep breath, she stood and made her way to the exit, casting one last glance over her shoulder at Donovan as the room emptied for a break.

She could feel her stomach rumbling, a reminder that the only thing she had eaten was the terrible turkey sandwich. She sat in the restaurant, which was completely deserted. Most of the guests were still in the banquet hall, and it was only 3:00. Sienna seated herself and looked at the menu absentmindedly.

"Is this seat taken?" a deep, familiar voice asked, startling her.

She looked up, her green eyes widening as they met the dark, intense gaze of Professor Hayes.

Instinctively, she jolted up from her seat.

"N-no," she stammered. "Do you need it?"

Donovan let out a hearty laugh.

"Well, I was going to join you for a moment."

Sienna sat slowly; her mouth open in awe. "Okay. Um, hi."

"I noticed you during the presentation," he said, his voice joyful. "You seemed quite ... engaged."

Sienna felt heat rising to her cheeks. Had she been that obvious? "It was fascinating," she managed.

Donovan smirked. "What are you planning to order?"

Sienna shrugged, "I dunno. Just killing time, I guess."

"Don't worry, you have plenty of time to decide, I imagine." Donovan chuckled softly.

"DONOVAN!" a voice boomed from across the restaurant.

"Ah, Dr. Emerson!" Donovan replied with zest.

"See you around." He placed a hand on Sienna's shoulder as he rose from his seat and walked off with his colleague.

Sienna giggled under her breath as she hid her blushing face behind the menu. She shifted in her seat as she waited for someone to appear and take her drink order.

"Ma'am?" A cook showing up for work broke the silence. "The restaurant doesn't open until five."

Flames of embarrassment rose and tingled on her cheeks. She quickly stood and ducked her head, trying to hide from the perceived scrutiny of judging eyes around her.

"I guess it's time for another turkey sandwich," she groaned as she made her way back to the prepackaged options. "Oh, look. Let's shake things up with chicken this time." She grabbed her sandwich and an expensive bottle of water and headed for the elevators.

Her heart pounded as she closed her hotel room door behind her, leaning against it with a shaky sigh. She kicked off her shoes and shuffled to the window, gazing out at the city.

"God, what am I doing here?" she whispered, her breath fogging the glass.

She closed her eyes, but all she could see was Professor Hayes at the podium, his deep voice resonating through her very core.

"This is insane," Sienna scolded herself, moving away from the window.

She needed a way to catch his attention. Idly watching him as he gave speeches and shook hands simply wasn't enough.

She decided to take a shower, hoping empty thoughts in the heat would help her brainstorm. The steam rose around her, curling against the glass shower door as beads of water slid down the surface.

Her thoughts began to spiral. She imagined Professor Hayes stepping into the shower with her, their bodies pressing against each other. She pictured his strong hands gripping the walls while he leaned closer to her wet skin.

Her fingers trailed down her body, mimicking the path she longed for his hands to take. She imagined his deep voice whispering praise in her ear, telling her how beautiful she was, how much he wanted her.

Sienna's hand dipped lower, her movements becoming more urgent as the fantasy intensified. She leaned against the cool tile wall, eyes closed tight as she lost herself.

As she imagined Donovan touching her, kissing her, pleasuring her, a bold and impulsive idea suddenly popped into her mind.

"I've got it!" Sienna's exclamation echoed in the shower.

Determined, she shut off the shower and dried off.

Glancing at the time on her phone, she saw it was 9:15. 'He'll be back soon,' she thought to herself as she quickly got dressed, slipping on delicate lace panties and a robe. She grabbed the hotel hair dryer and turned it on to the highest setting, urging the weak appliance to work faster. The strands of her hair flew wildly as she dried them, trying to tame them into place. The sound of the motor echoed through the empty room, accompanied by the faint smell of burnt hair. "Hurry up!" she yelled at the stubborn machine, desperate to finish getting ready.

She approached the door of her hotel room and turned the handle, manipulating the locks to leave it slightly open.

With a deep breath, she sat near the door, hidden from view but close enough to hear any noise from the hallway. Her ears were trained for the familiar chime of the elevator, signaling an arrival.

Time seemed to crawl by as Sienna waited, her heart beginning to relax with each passing moment. She hoped for some sort of confirmation that Professor Hayes would be coming down the hall to her. She remained vigilant, determined to wait as long as it took for him to arrive.

The silence was deafening, broken only by the occasional sound of the elevator or someone passing by in the hallway. Still, she waited, with nothing but anticipation and longing for his presence to keep her company.

Just as she was about to give up, the elevator let out one more chime. Her heart throbbed against her ribcage as she heard his deep voice issuing a polite goodnight to a colleague.

It was him. She quickly stood.

"Time for a show," she whispered to herself.

She peeled off the robe until she was clad only in those delicate panties. She ran her hands over her body, feeling the curves and dips of her skin, shaking out her long red hair, letting it cascade down her bare back.

She positioned herself directly in line with the hallway, her back to the door. Her porcelain skin glowed in the light that filtered in. The shape of her body was highlighted by the tight grip of her panties against her shapely backside. She could feel her heart racing, a mix of fear and exhilaration pulsing through her veins. Every beat sent a rush of adrenaline coursing through her, heightening her senses and sharpening her focus on what was to come.

"What if it's not him?" she thought. But the danger only heightened her arousal.

She listened intently, waiting for his footsteps outside her door, his cologne in the air. Would he stop? Would he look? The anticipation was delicious torture.

The sound of approaching footsteps made Sienna grin with a seductive desire. Her heart pounded as they grew closer.

Closer.

Even closer.

They paused just outside her door.

Sandalwood and tobacco—the spicy, masculine cologne tickling her nose confirmed his arrival.

Professor Hayes.

Sienna's skin tingled, hyper-aware of her exposed state. She allowed her professor to enjoy her backside, her luscious red hair falling to just above her waist. She turned slightly, giving the barest glimpse of the side of her breast. The silence stretched, thick with tension.

Then, a deliberate clearing of a throat.

"Ahem."

His low, rich voice elicited a shiver from Sienna. She smoothly drifted towards her nightstand, giving him one final alluring glimpse before disappearing from view.

His footsteps resumed, continuing down the hall to his own room. The soft clicks of his door opening, then closing, echoed in the silence.

Sienna leaned against the wall, her legs trembling. "Holy shit," she whispered, a giddy laugh bubbling up.

Her skin felt electric, every nerve ending alive with sensation. She hurriedly pulled back on the robe, her mind racing. She ran to the door, quickly securing it.

Sprawled out on the bed, she waited patiently for Donovan's response. Would he call her room? Knock on the door? It was his move, and she eagerly awaited it.

Her heart raced as she replayed the moment over and over in her mind. Every detail was etched into her memory, fueling her anticipation. She imagined Donovan pacing in his room, wrestling with the decision of whether to call on her.

She picked up the hotel phone, wrestling with the thought of calling him.

"No," she stopped herself. "It's his move."

She considered texting him.

"AAAHHH! This is crazy!"

She flopped back on the bed, turning on the TV.

The flickering light of the television caused her eyelids to grow heavy.

She whispered his name, "Donovan," a sweet caress on her lips as her eyes finally closed.

In her dreams, strong hands caressed her skin, leaving trails of fire in their wake. Dark eyes gazed into hers, full of intensity and unspoken desire. The scent of his cologne enveloped her, spicy and intoxicating.

The Card

The shrill beep of her alarm jolted her awake. Disoriented, she blinked at the sunlight streaming through the curtains.

It suddenly dawned on her. Donovan didn't call. He didn't knock. She checked her cell phone only to find it absent of notifications.

Did he not like what he saw? What it if wasn't even him? Her mind raced with thoughts of defeat and embarrassment.

The rumbling of her stomach snapped her out of her thoughts. She had forgotten to eat dinner in her excitement, and now she was feeling the consequences. She didn't want to go to the restaurant, afraid that Donovan would be there, but she had no choice. She couldn't make sense of his reaction, or lack thereof, and it left her feeling uneasy.

She slowly dressed, her stomach a knot of anticipation as she made her way to the restaurant. The sounds of cutlery and conversation washed over her as she entered.

And then she saw him.

Professor Hayes sat at a table surrounded by his colleagues. His mere presence demanded attention, even in this informal environment. His gaze briefly met hers. She detected a hint of something, but then he looked away, engrossed in a text message that had just come through on his phone.

Deflated, Sienna found a solitary table in the corner. She didn't wait for a waiter to appear and headed immediately for the breakfast buffet. Doubt crept in as she served herself a plate of eggs.

"What was I thinking?" she whispered to herself, cheeks burning with embarrassment. "He probably thinks I'm some kind of ... of..."

The word "slut" hovered unspoken, a remnant of her conservative upbringing. She shook her head, trying to dispel the negative thoughts while walking back to her table.

Despite her growling stomach, she had no desire to eat. She took small bites, attempting to silence the grumbling in her belly, but not enough to truly satisfy her hunger.

Whispering to herself, she pushed her plate aside. "What would he want with a college kid, anyway?" Feeling embarrassed and close to tears, she hastily got up and made her way back to her room.

Her hand trembled as she slid her keycard into the lock. The soft click echoed in the empty hallway as she pushed open the door, her mind already racing with plans to pack her bags and leave.

She walked into her room and froze.

Lying on top of the rumpled white duvet was a solitary red rose. Beside it, an envelope.

Sienna approached the bed with tentative steps. She lifted the envelope, inhaling the fragrance of the rose still resting on the bed. Inside, she found a small card bearing three simple words in an elegant script:

"I see you."

A strangled gasp escaped her lips as something else fell from the envelope—a room key. Attached to it was a small note: "Ten pm."

Sienna sank onto the bed, her legs suddenly weak.

"Oh, shit," she whispered under her breath.

A flood of emotions washed over her—excitement, fear, and an overwhelming surge of desire. Her imagination ran wild, conjuring vivid scenarios of what might await her that evening.

She closed her eyes, picturing Professor Hayes' strong hands on her skin, his deep voice in her ear. In her mind, he pushed her against the wall, his body pressing urgently against hers. She imagined his lips trailing down her neck, his fingers tangling in her hair.

"Professor," she breathed, her cheeks flushing hot with the forbidden nature of her fantasies.

Her eyes snapped open, her breath coming in short, sharp gasps. The reality of what lay ahead both thrilled and terrified her. As she clutched the room key to her chest, one thought echoed through her mind:

"What have I done?"

She smoothed her blouse and prepared to attend the day's events at the conference. Her reflection in the mirror stared back at her, wide-eyed and flushed.

The banquet hall buzzed with activity as Sienna entered, her eyes darting nervously around the room. She approached the large schedule board, scanning for Professor Hayes' name. Her heart sank when she found no trace of him listed for the day's events.

She let out a soft whisper of frustration. "What the hell do I do now?"

With no other plans and limited funds, she was stuck.

"Looks like I'll just be in here today."

Sienna found herself struggling to focus on the presentations. Her mind kept drifting to the room key burning a hole in her pocket and the promise of 10:00 PM.

The afternoon arrived, bringing with it an awards ceremony. Sienna sat near the back, her eyes constantly searching the crowd. Just as she was about to give up hope, a familiar figure entered the hall.

Professor Hayes strode in, commanding attention without even trying. He was dressed flawlessly in a dark suit.

"Oh God," Sienna thought, her heart pounding. "He's here. He's still here."

She couldn't tear her eyes away from him. Every movement, every subtle gesture, seemed to speak directly to her. The anticipation of what was to come later that night left her dizzy with desire and fear.

He made his way along the back of the room, careful not to disturb the ongoing presentations. The soft rustle of his suit jacket against the fabric of the chairs seemed impossibly loud to Sienna's hypersensitive ears.

He chose a seat directly behind her, just close enough for her to feel his gaze pressing into her. Her ponytail left her succulent neck on display for him.

Award presentations continued, seemingly forever. Donovan leaned in.

"I trust you found my little gift," his voice was like velvet.

She nodded quickly, not daring to turn to face him. Her skin tingled where his breath had ghosted over it.

"Good," he continued, a hint of amusement in his tone. "I look forward to our ... discussion later."

With that, he leaned back in his chair, leaving Sienna flushed and trembling. She tried to focus on the speaker at the podium, but the words washed over her without registering.

The master of ceremonies stepped up to the podium for the final award, his voice echoing through the hall. "And now, for the Distinguished Contribution to Historical Studies award, we are honored to present it to Professor Donovan Hayes."

A smattering of applause filled the air as Hayes rose from his seat, buttoning his suit jacket with an effortless grace. He walked to the stage, his strides long and confident.

His deep voice reverberated through the microphone. "Thank you. This recognition is truly humbling."

Sienna leaned forward in her chair, hanging on his every word. His speech was eloquent, peppered with historical references and dry humor that had the audience chuckling appreciatively. But it was his next action that sent her heart into overdrive.

Mid-sentence, Hayes' eyes landed directly on Sienna. The corner of his mouth quirked up, and he winked at her.

Her face turned red with a sudden rush of heat. "Did he really just...?" she wondered, her thoughts spinning wildly. "In front of everyone?"

As the event reached its end, Sienna quietly exited the ballroom. Her legs trembled as she walked to the elevator, her mind racing with ideas, wants, and worries.

"Ten pm," she whispered to herself as the elevator doors closed. "What am I going to do?"

Her hands shook as she rifled through her suitcase. 'What does one wear to a rendezvous with her professor?' she wondered, holding up various items of clothing. The anticipation was almost unbearable, a mix of excitement and trepidation coursing through her veins.

She took a deep breath as the clock struck the designated hour, preparing herself for what was to come. She rummaged through her suitcase and found some ancient breath freshener, its flavor almost pure alcohol. "It's time," she whispered to herself before grabbing the door handle. "Here we go."

Whiskey

Sienna's fingers trembled against the cool metal handle as she peered into Professor Hayes' darkened suite. His silhouette greeted her, a dark figure outlined against the white window shade. He sat regally in the standard-issue hotel office chair, his posture radiating confidence and control. One leg crossed over the other, he exuded an air of sophistication and poise. His neatly pressed shirt covered his chest, with three buttons left open to reveal a hint of toned muscle. The rich scents of sandalwood and tobacco filled her senses, wrapping around her like a warm embrace. She knew it to be his signature scent that always lingered after he was gone.

"Come in, Miss Holloway," he beckoned.

Sienna hesitated. She smoothed her simple blouse, suddenly aware of how plain she must look. With measured steps, she entered, closing the door behind her with a noticeable click.

The room was awash with hues of amber, the only color coming from the sloshing liquid in Donovan's tumbler. The rich hues of the whiskey danced across his salt-and-pepper beard, casting warm highlights in its wake. The scent was heavy with the smell of aged oak and a hint of vanilla. Donovan brought the glass to his lips and savored the smooth aroma as he took a slow sip.

"He's so fucking hot," she thought, heat rising to her cheeks.

"You're right on time," Hayes said, his eyes roaming over her with quiet intensity. "I appreciate punctuality."

"Th-thank you, Professor," Sienna stammered. She took another tentative step forward, drawn by some unseen force.

The room seemed to shrink; the air growing thick and heady. Sienna's fingers fidgeted as she struggled to maintain composure.

Donovan's lips curved into a subtle smile. "Stand there for a moment. Just like that," he commanded.

Sienna's breath quickened, her mind racing with possibilities. She remained frozen, caught between desire, uncertainty, and submission.

"What can I do for you, Professor?" She asked, both thrilled and terrified by the answer.

The Professor's dark eyes held Sienna's gaze; his expression unreadable. "Let's discuss your performance in class, shall we?" His deep voice resonated through the dim room, commanding yet tinged with warmth.

Sienna stood there, still, her hands clasped tightly in front of her. "Of course, Professor," she meekly replied.

"Your essays show remarkable insight," Hayes began, leaning forward slightly. "However, your reluctance to speak up in discussions is prohibitive."

Sienna's cheeks flushed with a mix of pride and embarrassment. "I … I'm sorry," she whispered, her eyes downcast. "I guess I'm not that confident."

Donovan's voice softened. "There's no need to apologize, Ms. Holloway. Your intelligence is evident. I simply want to see you shine."

Sienna glanced up, meeting his intense gaze. "Thank you," she breathed. "That means a lot."

Gathering her courage, Sienna continued, her voice trembling slightly. "Actually, Professor Hayes, I've been meaning to tell you … I admire your teaching style. The way you bring history to life is … inspiring."

Donovan's eyebrow arched, his ego flickering in his eyes. "Oh? Do tell me more."

Her fingers twisted nervously. "I—I saw you'd be speaking at the conference. That's why I decided to attend."

The admission hung in the air between them, charged with unspoken implications. Sienna's heart pounded; her vulnerability laid bare.

Donovan leaned back in his chair, his gaze lingering on Sienna's face. The dim light accentuated the sharp angles of his jaw.

"I see," his voice dropping to a seductive timbre. "Your fascination is ... intriguing, Sienna."

"And my teaching style, is that the only reason you decided to attend the conference this weekend?" He stood slowly and took another sip from his golden elixir.

"N—no," Sienna stammered. "Not quite."

"Your hotel room?" His voice boomed with an authoritative edge, his eyes piercing into Sienna's soul. "Is it just a coincidence that our doors happen to be separated by a mere thirty feet?"

Sienna's heart raced as she remained silent, unsure if she was being reprimanded or if her professor was impressed with her diligence. The weight of his gaze felt like a physical force, pushing her down and suffocating her. She could feel herself shrinking under his scrutiny, the silence between them deafening. It was as if he could see through every thought and emotion in her mind, leaving her feeling exposed and vulnerable.

His fingers traced the smooth rim of his whiskey glass. The liquid inside swirled gently as he spoke. "I see," his voice low and smooth.

"There's a certain ... complexity to our relationship, wouldn't you agree?" His tone was laced with a hint of amusement as he tilted his head thoughtfully.

Sienna's chest rose and fell rapidly beneath her simple blouse. She felt pinned by Donovan's intense gaze, like a butterfly on display.

"I ... yes," she breathed, her submissive nature emerging in response to his commanding presence. Her voice grew softer, more timid.

Hayes leaned forward, the movement slow and deliberate. "And how does that make you feel, Ms. Holloway?"

Sienna's lips parted, her mind reeling. She wanted to surrender, to give in to the magnetic pull between them, but a tiny voice in the back of her mind whispered caution.

"It's ... overwhelming," she sighed, her fingers twisting in her hands. "Thrilling and scary at the same time."

He set his glass down with a soft clink, the sound echoing in the charged silence between them as he slowly stood.

"Overwhelming," he repeated, savoring the word. "Yes, I can imagine it would be. Especially for someone like you, Sienna."

Her cheeks flushed deeper, a rosy hue spreading down her neck. "Someone like me?" she echoed.

Hayes slowly approached her, his voice dropping. "Someone so ... responsive. So attuned to every subtle shift in mood and desire."

She took in his word—desire. The anticipation lingered in her mind, thrilling her with possibilities. She could almost taste the vanilla whiskey on his lips, so close yet still maddeningly out of reach.

His eyes roamed over her flushed face, tracing the faint outline of her jaw and the curve of her lips. His voice was smooth and seductive, laced with a hint of taboo. "I can't help but wonder," he mused, "if you've ever truly succumbed to the intoxicating rush of surrendering control."

She could feel the allure and danger of what he was offering, and a thrill ran through her at the thought of giving in to him completely.

A soft gasp escaped Sienna's parted lips. Her heart raced as images flashed through her mind - his strong hands as they trailed over her skin, igniting a fire within her. She squirmed restlessly, her body tense with anticipation and desire. The sensation between her thighs only intensified. Every inch of her craved his touch, his kiss, his passion.

Her voice trembled as she admitted, "No ... I've never... thought about it." Her heart raced with fear and curiosity as Donovan's smile deepened, his eyes glinting with a dangerous satisfaction. "Oh, Sienna," he breathed, inching closer. "The pleasures I could show you..." She swallowed hard, her mind reeling with possibilities.

Her heart thundered in her chest, her breath coming in shallow pants. She trembled as she took a hesitant step towards her professor.

"Professor," she whispered, her voice quivering. "I ... I want..."

Donovan's eyes darkened, his gaze intense as he watched her approach. "What do you want, Ms. Holloway?" he asked, his voice low and commanding.

She swallowed hard, gathering her courage. "You," she breathed. "I want you."

His movements were deliberate and controlled as he closed the distance between them. Sienna retreated instinctively, finding her back against the wall. Suddenly, he was there, his body pressing against hers, his hands braced on either side of her waist.

His breath was hot against her ear. "Are you okay?"

Sienna nodded, unable to form words as his hands began to roam. His touch was both tender and possessive, igniting sensations she had never experienced before.

"Yes," Sienna gasped, arching into his touch. "Please, Professor. I'm..."

Donovan's lips met hers in an intense, passionate kiss, his desire and appetite unmistakable.

Smoldering with passion, Sienna was consumed by him, her body responding with an unexpected intensity. She yielded completely to his dominant touch, her fingers gripping his shirt as she pulled him closer, desperate for more of his intoxicating presence.

Donovan's words whispered against her lips, "Good girl."

Donovan's hands roamed her body, his touch igniting a fire within her. She moaned softly, her hips arching towards him in an unconscious invitation for more.

He whispered in her ear, "I love the way you taste."

Sienna nodded eagerly. "Thank you, sir."

"Now," he demanded, his voice harsh and commanding, "show me what you were hiding last night." Donovan stalked backwards until his foot reached the edge of the bed. His glass was firmly gripped in one hand while the other steadied his descent on the mattress. He sat, watching, taking a deep swig of whiskey that burned down his throat with a spicy passion.

Sienna began to unbutton her blouse in a hurried fashion, eager to keep Donovan's attention.

"Slowly, slowly," Donovan directed, speaking in a low, yet controlling tone.

She did as she was told and finished unbuttoning her blouse, revealing a velvety black bra underneath. Donovan's eyes grew wide with anticipation. He took another sip of his whiskey, savoring the taste as he watched her every move.

Sienna's breasts were full and round, straining against the delicate fabric of her bra. She slowly unhooked it, exposing her breasts to his gaze. Donovan's eyes traced the outlines of her nipples as they hardened under his intense stare.

She turned around; her legs were almost too weak to hold her up. Slowly, she let her skirt fall to the floor, revealing a matching pair of panties that gave just a hint of her butt cheek exposed.

"Exquisite," He proclaimed. "Now, face me."

Sienna obliged.

"Such a pretty girl."

There was a heavy pause as Donovan reviewed the specimen before him.

"On your knees." His words were low, soft, yet intoxicating. "Crawl towards me, slowly."

She followed his command without question as Donovan rose to his feet. She felt like a mere puppet under his control, feeling his power over her as reveled in the submission.

At last, she reached his feet and looked up at him expectantly, waiting for his next command. His eyes hungrily took in every inch of her exposed skin as she presented herself to him.

"You are mine now," he said with a wicked grin.

He loomed over her, a towering figure of dominance and power. Sienna's eyes were drawn to the undeniable bulge in his pants, her heart racing with anticipation and fear. She knew her place, and every instinct in her body screamed for his approval. Donovan held her captive with just a touch of his thumb against her soft cheeks, relishing in the control he had over her. He wanted the tension to build, to see her eagerness grow until she was practically quivering with desire.

"May I, Professor?" Sienna asked as she placed her delicate fingers on his belt buckle.

With a single nod and a wicked grin, he gave silent permission.

Her fingers trembled as she struggled to undo the buckle. Donovan's deep chuckle taunted her, "Hurry up, pretty girl." Sienna blushed but was too focused on freeing his erection from its confines. With each tug of the zipper, she could feel his throbbing manhood straining against the fabric. Finally, with a triumphant gasp, she released the restraints and his thick, pulsing member sprang forth, ready for her touch.

His pants immediately dropped to the floor, exposing thighs that were thick and muscular, tapering down to defined calves that spoke of hours spent running or cycling. His legs were coated in a delicate layer of dark hair, emphasizing the strong contours and dips of his muscular physique.

Sienna's heart raced as she held her new treasure in her hands, eager to explore and tantalize. She traced her fingers over every inch, feeling the heat emanating from its surface. She leaned in to give gentle kisses and licks, both craving each other more with each touch. She slowly took his cock into her mouth, sucking on it softly at first, savoring the taste and texture. Donovan groaned loudly, his body jolting with pleasure as he entered her.

His fingers tangled in her silky hair. He guided her movements, setting the pace. Her tongue swirled around his shaft, tracing every vein and ridge. She hollowed her cheeks, creating a delicious suction that made him groan deeply.

Sienna tilted her head back and gazed up at him with a coy expression, her eyes glittering with eagerness to please. He relished in the sight of her lips wrapped tightly around him. He guided her face further onto his cock, encouraging her to consume him even deeper.

She relaxed her throat, allowing him to slide in further. The tip of his cock pushed back enough to make her eyes water, but she didn't pull away, determined to take all of him. Her hands caressed his thighs, feeling the muscles tense beneath her fingertips.

Donovan's hips began to move, thrusting gently into her willing mouth. He set a steady rhythm, his breathing growing ragged. Sienna matched his pace, her head bobbing in time with his thrusts.

She intensified her movements, using her tongue and lips in a frenzy of passion to bring him to the brink of ecstasy. Each suck and kiss were executed with such precision that he was quickly lost in waves of pleasure, teetering on the edge of release.

His grip tightened in her hair as he struggled to hold back, but the intensity of her actions made it almost impossible to resist any longer. Every sensation was heightened, every touch electric with desire as she skillfully brought him closer and closer to the ultimate climax.

With a voice like thunder, he commanded, "Get on your feet," as he unbuttoned his shirt. The urge to unleash his passion coursed through him, but he wanted to prolong the game with his new toy. Deep down, he relished the adrenaline rush of anticipation just as much.

Sienna rose slowly to her feet, feeling both vulnerable and powerful at the same time. She caressed her nipples as she waited for his next move. He circled her slowly, almost predatory, taking in every angle of her almost-naked form.

Donovan sat back down on the bed, pulling Sienna towards him. "You're beautiful," he growled, before leaning in to capture one taut nipple between his lips. She arched into him, moaning as he teased it with his tongue and teeth. He trailed kisses down her stomach, stopping just above the panties that had taunted him just moments ago. His hands caressed down her delicate back as he reached further down, pulling her panties off with one smooth motion.

She looked at him with a mixture of fear and desire in her eyes. Without warning, he jolted up, spun her around and pushed her onto the bed, pinning her beneath him.

She squirmed beneath him, but it only fueled Donovan's lust even more. He kissed her neck passionately, nipping at her flesh as he made his way down to her exposed breasts. He took a hardened nipple into his mouth, sucking on it hungrily as he rolled it between his teeth.

Donovan's breathing quickened in anticipation of the forbidden pleasure that awaited him. Her legs were parted, inviting him in with a delicious vulnerability. Their gazes locked, filled with a primal hunger that threatened to consume them both.

His fingers traced the outline of her pussy, teasing her as he felt the heat emanating from her core. She was dripping wet with anticipation.

Sienna's breath shortened as Donovan's fingers worked their magic inside her. Her hips rocked against his hand, desperate for more friction. Soft whimpers escaped her lips as waves of pleasure radiated through her body.

"That's it, pretty girl," Donovan approved. "Let go for me."

His thumb found her clit, circling it with expert precision. Sienna's back arched off the bed, her fingers twisting in the sheets. She was close, teetering on the edge of ecstasy.

"Please," she gasped. "Professor, I need..."

"What do you need?" Donovan growled, increasing the pressure. "Tell me."

"You," Sienna moaned. "Get inside me. Please..."

Donovan forcefully removed his dripping fingers from Sienna's trembling body, eliciting a bratty whimper from her lips. He pressed his two fingers against her mouth, parting her supple lips and forcing them open to taste the forbidden nectar that her young body had produced. Their mouths met in a heated kiss, tongues dueling for dominance as the scent of his cologne mingled with the intoxicating taste of her pussy and his whiskey.

Sienna gasped as he pushed himself into her. She wrapped her legs around him instinctively, urging him deep.

"You're exquisite. So responsive, so eager to please. Such a good little girl."

He began moving slowly at first, his hips thrusting in a sensual rhythm that had Sienna panting for air. He teased and tormented her with each stroke, building the tension until she thought she might explode from the need for release.

She clutched at his shoulders tightly, digging her nails into his skin as she threw back her head and let out a loud, primal scream.

Donovan responded by picking up speed, pounding into her with a force that left no doubt about who was in control. His hips slapped against hers repeatedly as they both lost themselves in the sensation. They moved together seamlessly, their bodies becoming one entwined entity, moving only towards one goal: their orgasms.

Waves of pleasure crashed over Sienna as she clung to Donovan, her body trembling in their passionate encounter. Her skin was flushed and glistening with a light sheen of sweat.

She wrapped her arms around his neck, pulling him closer as their lips met in a fiery kiss. Their tongues tangled and danced, teasing each other with quick flicks and long strokes.

"Fuck me," she panted. "Fill me up."

Donovan growled in response, hips pounding against hers in a rhythmic pattern. Her inner walls tightened around him, massaging his cock with a sense of urgency that matched his own.

"Oh, does the pretty girl enjoy that?" he growled, his eyes burning with unrestrained lust.

"Yes," she moaned, her body trembling with need. "More. Harder."

He pulled back slightly before slamming into her again, hitting her sweet spot with precision. Sienna cried out loudly, her body convulsing from the overwhelming pleasure that radiated through her core. She writhed beneath him, lost in the sensations that consumed every fiber of her being.

The room was filled with the sounds of skin smacking against skin and the scent of sweat filling the air, making it almost too thick to breathe.

With a powerful thrust, Donovan drove himself deeper into Sienna's pulsing little pussy. She let out a guttural moan, her body trembling as pleasure surged through every nerve. Her fingers dug into his back, holding onto him as she rode the wave of ecstasy he had ignited within her.

"God," he groaned, feeling her walls clench around him. "You're fucking gorgeous. I love it when you cum for me."

He gave one final push, burying himself to the hilt within her.

"Fill me!" Sienna cried out.

Donovan held himself up on one arm, his gaze locked with Sienna's. He squeezed her cheeks, forcefully opening her lips as he spat into her mouth.

"You filthy little slut."

"Yes, sir."

His hand came down in a stinging slap against her cheek, eliciting a soft whimper from Sienna.

"Thank you, Professor."

The headboard crashed loudly against the wall as Donovan continued his unrelenting assault on her dripping arousal. The rhythmic thumping of their bodies echoed through the room, accompanied by the moans and gasps of their mutual pleasure.

"I'm going to fill your fucking hole."

"Please, Professor. Please fill me. I've earned it."

Donovan's pace became frenzied, his hips pistoning against Sienna's with increasing urgency. Sweat glistened on his brow, droplets cascading down the planes of his chiseled chest. The muscles in his arms and back rippled with each powerful thrust, testament to the raw strength he was unleashing upon her willing body.

"That's it," he growled, his voice rough with exertion and arousal. "Take all of me, you greedy little whore."

Donovan's entire body tensed as his climax overtook him. A primal groan tore from his throat. His cock pulsed powerfully inside Sienna, each throb sending spurts of hot seed deep into her welcoming depths.

The sensation was overwhelming—pure, unadulterated bliss radiating from his core and spreading like wildfire through every nerve ending. His muscles spasmed and his vision blurred, the world narrowing to nothing but the exquisite feeling of release.

Sienna lay beneath him as she basked in the intense encounter. Donovan collapsed onto her chest, their sweaty bodies sticking together in a tangled mess of limbs and fulfilled desires.

Donovan's strong arms enveloped her, pulling her close against his chest. His heartbeat thundered beneath her ear, gradually slowing to a steady rhythm. The scent of sandalwood and tobacco enveloped her, mingling with the heady aroma of their lovemaking.

"Thank you, sir."

"How are you feeling?" he whispered.

"Mmm," Sienna sighed contentedly. "A little sore, but in the best way."

"Good. You were magnificent," his lips brushing against her temple.

She nuzzled closer, basking in the afterglow. She felt safe and utterly satisfied in a way she had never experienced before. A contented sigh escaped her lips as she savored the warmth of his embrace.

She slowly rose from the bed and made her way to the bathroom, phone in hand, like most college students.

Standing in front of the mirror, she scrolled through her phone, getting lost in the mundane.

Her phone buzzed. It was a message from Donovan:

"Are you alright?"

Her heart raced as she typed and erased dozens of responses before settling on a simple, "Yes. You?"

The ellipsis appeared and disappeared several times before his reply came through: "Conflicted. But I had fun."

She closed her eyes, overwhelmed by the flood of emotions his words evoked. The thrill of their shared desire warred with the anxiety of potential consequences.

"What happens now?" she typed, her finger hovering over the send button for a long moment before she gathered the courage to press it.

Donovan's response was quick this time. "We'll see. Come back to bed."

Sienna obeyed; her body sated but her mind buzzing with conflicting thoughts. Her heart, mind, and body were at war, and she didn't know how to find peace between them.

Checking Out

T he soft morning light filtered in, casting a warm glow across Sienna's bare skin. She stirred, her eyes fluttering open to find Donovan's gentle gaze fixed upon her. A blush crept across her cheeks as memories of their passionate night flooded back.

"Good morning," Donovan's voice slowly warming from his slumber.

Sienna's heart raced as she sat upright in bed, pulling the crumpled sheets up to her chest. She looked around the room, scanning for her scattered clothing. "I should probably get dressed," she said in a hushed tone.

Donovan's hand on her arm stopped her. "There's no rush," his tone gentle yet commanding. "The conference is over. We have all the time in the world."

His fingertips traced along her skin, igniting a craving that she couldn't deny. Her body trembled with anticipation, but her mind fought against the temptation. There was the possibility that his actions the previous evening were merely fueled by the whiskey he consumed.

"But..." she whispered, struggling to form a coherent thought as he leaned in closer, his intoxicating scent enveloping her senses.

"Stay," Donovan insisted. "Let's order room service. Enjoy our morning together. What would you like for breakfast?"

Sienna, her heart racing, had never ordered room service before. Her voice shook as she stammered out an answer. "Um, just some fruit and coffee, please." The word 'coffee' felt foreign on her tongue. She was used to indulging in sugary drinks from the campus coffee bar, and wasn't sure what to expect from room service delivery. She felt a twinge of embarrassment at her simple order, but also a strong need to impress the man lying in bed next to her.

Donovan let out a short, hearty chuckle, seeing right through her attempt to seem nonchalant. "Bacon or sausage?" he asked with a playful smile. Sienna shrugged, trying not to show how flustered she was by his charm.

"Uh, sausage, I guess." Her stomach grumbled in agreement.

"Yeah, we both know how you like sausage," he said with a playful glint in his eye.

"There's a nightgown for you," Donovan tilted his head toward the desk as he pressed the hotel phone to his ear. "I was hoping you'd still be here in the morning, so I picked it up yesterday before the ceremony."

Sienna's eyes widened in shock and appreciation. The nightgown was a soft, pastel pink, adorned with intricate lace.

She tiptoed out of the warm bed and padded across the room, her skin prickling under Donovan's intense stare. Slipping the gown over her head, she twirled around the room in a playful dance, admiring her reflection in the mirror. "You have such great taste," she said to Donovan with a radiant smile as he finalized their breakfast order and hung up the phone.

The whisper-soft fabric clung to her curves, the hemline brushing mid-thigh. Though it covered her, the thin straps and plunging neckline left little to the imagination.

"Donovan," she began, blushing, her voice hesitant and embarrassed. "I can't find my panties from last night."

A grin spread across his lips as he replied, "I know."

A blush of pink spread across her cheeks, a mixture of confusion and amusement evident in her expression. "Are you hiding them from me?"

His eyes sparkled. "I don't want you wearing any. Besides, you look ravishing."

Sienna watched, mesmerized, as Donovan pulled on a pair of loose cotton shorts and a t-shirt. Her eyes traced the strong planes of his bare chest, lingering on the trail of dark hair disappearing beneath the waistband. She swallowed hard, realizing he, himself, had forgone underwear.

Donovan moved towards her with confident steps, his muscular frame drawing her in close as he pulled her against him. She melted into his embrace, savoring the sensation of his warm skin against her own. She let go of her usual nerves and self-doubt, allowing herself to fully immerse in the moment.

Her fingers traced the contours of his chest, her touch feather-light and hesitant. She marveled at the contrast between his tanned skin and her pale hand, feeling the steady thrum of his heartbeat beneath her palm.

"You're trembling," he observed, his breath hot against her ear. "Are you cold?"

She shook her head, her silky red hair brushing against his chin. "No, I'm just ... overwhelmed. This feels like a dream."

Donovan chuckled softly, the sound reverberating through his chest. "I can assure you, it's very real." His hand slid down her back, fingers tracing the curve of her spine through the delicate fabric of the nightgown.

A sharp knock at the door jolted Sienna from her reverie. She stepped back from Donovan, smoothing her nightgown with trembling hands.

"Room service," a muffled voice called.

Donovan moved to answer, holding the door open as the waiter pushed in his cart. Sienna was caught off guard by another conversation at the door. Dr. Emerson, wheeling his luggage down the hall, stopped for a brief chat.

"Professor Hayes, what a fantastic presentation!" Emerson proclaimed.

"Thank you, thank you," replied Hayes as Dr. Emerson quickly glanced in the room.

The elderly man's eyes widened in surprise, his gaze raking over Sienna's form before quickly darting away. She stood in the back of the room, her curves accentuated by the delicate fabric and skin shimmering under the lights. His reaction was a mix of shock and embarrassment, as if he had stumbled upon something forbidden and alluring at the same time.

"I'm sorry, I didn't mean to interrupt," explained Dr. Emerson as he shook Donovan's hand with a polite smile, stealing one last glance at Sienna before continuing down the hall.

Sienna felt her cheeks burn, acutely aware of how this must look.

Donovan shut the door behind the waiter as he left. He turned to Sienna, his expression a mix of concern and resignation.

"Are you alright?" he asked softly.

Sienna nodded, wrapping her arms around herself. "Do you think he recognized me?"

Donovan shook his head. "He doesn't know you as a student of mine. I don't think any harm was done, but it does force us to discuss our dynamic."

The weight of their situation settled over them like a heavy blanket. Sienna sank onto the edge of the bed, her earlier confidence evaporating.

"What are we going to do?" she whispered.

Donovan sat beside her, his hand resting on her thigh, briefly comforting her.

"This is about more than just our reputations, Sienna. What happened between us ... it's new territory for me. And I have to admit, I had fun observing you this weekend."

"Wait, you watched me?" Sienna asked in surprise.

"Of course. I saw you at the valet. I watched you check-in. I witnessed your pacing of the hotel grounds before my presentation."

Sienna's eyes widened, a mix of shock and intrigue flickering across her face. "I had no idea," her mind racing back to those moments, reimagining them with Donovan's watchful gaze upon her.

"You're captivating, Sienna. The way you move, the way you blush when you're nervous or embarrassed ... I couldn't look away."

His words made her heart race, a warmth spreading through her body. She leaned into him slightly, drawn to his magnetism. "And what did you see?"

"I saw a young woman trying so hard to appear confident and sophisticated. But underneath that facade, I saw your vulnerability, your eagerness to please." His hand moved higher up her thigh, pushing the hem of her nightgown up ever so slightly. "It was ... intoxicating."

Her skin tingled.

"So, now what?" she asked.

Hayes took a moment to compose himself before responding. "To start," he explained calmly. "Let's keep our classroom time strictly for classwork. There won't be any special treatment or favors, and we will maintain our roles as professor and pupil. Any other situations can be discussed as they arise, but let's not give anyone cause for suspicion."

"That's going to be hard," she rebutted. "You're just so ... yummy." Her eyes roamed over his muscular frame.

His hand tightened on her thigh. "Yummy, am I?" He leaned in closer. "You have no idea how delicious you look right now."

Sienna shivered, her body responding to his proximity. The thin fabric of her nightgown suddenly felt like too much, yet not enough. She longed to feel his skin against hers again.

"Maybe we should eat before the food gets cold," she suggested weakly, her resolve crumbling under his intense gaze.

Donovan nodded but made no move to pull away. "Of course," he agreed, his tone deceptively casual. "We wouldn't want to waste such a lovely breakfast."

He stood, moving to the cart laden with covered dishes. Sienna watched, mesmerized, as he lifted the silver domes to reveal steaming plates of eggs, sausages, and fresh fruit.

The aroma of fresh coffee and warm pastries began to fill the room, gradually easing the tension.

Donovan poured two cups of coffee.

"How would you like your coffee, pretty girl?"

Sienna froze, embarrassed.

"Um, I'm more of a vanilla latte kind of girl."

Donovan let out a chuckle. "I see. Well, that's okay. Maybe one day you'll enjoy actual coffee."

"No thanks," Sienna rebutted. "I love myself too much to submit my mouth to burnt bean water. But that fruit looks pretty good."

Her appetite returned as her nerves began to settle. She reached for a ripe strawberry, bringing it to her lips with deliberate slowness.

Donovan's eyes followed the movement, watching her take a delicate bite.

"Delicious," she teased.

As if reading her thoughts, Donovan leaned forward and kissed her neck.

"Sienna," Donovan breathed, his eyes intense. "You're exquisite."

She felt a blush creep up her neck, her natural shyness warring with the desire coursing through her veins. "Professor," she whispered, falling back on formality as her heart raced. The title dripped with dominance, its erotic undertones igniting a fiery passion within her.

"Professor." He grinned, his hand sliding up her thigh. "I like the authority that holds."

In one fluid motion, he pulled her onto his lap, his lips capturing hers in a searing kiss. Her hands tangled in his hair as she returned the kiss with equal fervor. The room became filled with the sounds of their ragged breathing and soft moans of pleasure.

Donovan's voice was low and husky as he pressed his lips against the sensitive skin of Sienna's neck. "I need you," he growled, his fingers digging into her hips.

Sienna arched towards him in response. "Shower," she moaned, as she started pulling him in the direction of the bathroom.

Donovan's muscles bulged as he effortlessly lifted Sienna into his arms, carrying her to the bathroom. Her legs instinctively wrapped around his waist.

The cool tiles beneath offered no relief from the scorching heat radiating between them as Donovan set her down gently.

She reached for the hem of her nightgown, but Donovan stopped her with a firm grip on her wrist. "No," he growled. "I want to reveal you." He slowly peeled away the thin fabric, each movement deliberate and intense, revealing her soft, pale skin inch by tantalizing inch.

As the shower hissed to life, steam began to fill the room, quickly turning into a thick, misty fog that surrounded them. Donovan stepped under the pounding spray, pulling Sienna close behind him. Water cascaded over their bodies, heightening every sensation, blurring the lines between pleasure and pain.

"You're mine," Donovan declared possessively as he claimed her lips in a kiss. Sienna moaned against his mouth, her body pulsing with desire as he explored every inch of her porcelain skin with his hands and mouth.

Sienna's usual shyness was replaced by an insatiable hunger for this man who knew how to push all her buttons and drive her wild.

Her hands explored Donovan's broad chest. She reveled in the contrast between his firm body and her soft curves.

He moved with purpose, finding her most sensitive spots and teasing them with expert touches and strokes. Her body arched and trembled, each sensation intensifying as he reached between them to find her most delicate nub. With skilled fingers, he rubbed it in slow, deliberate circles, sending waves of electricity through her. She moaned loudly into his mouth, her hips moving in unison with his fingers.

Sienna felt herself being lifted, her back pressed against the cool tiles. She wrapped her legs around Donovan's waist, gasping as he entered her. Donovan's hard member was thrust into her wet, tight pussy. Her high-pitched moans echoed off the tiled walls of the shower as he pressed her against the cold surface. Sienna's fingers clasped tightly into Donovan's muscular shoulders, her nails digging in as she cried out his title in pleasure.

"Fuck me, Professor!"

His thrusts were rhythmic and deep. She could feel every inch of him inside her, stretching and filling her. The contrast of his hot, hard length against her soft, yielding flesh was exquisite.

Sienna's hips bucked wildly, her climax building up inside her like a tidal wave. Donovan felt it too, feeling the telltale signs of her pending orgasmic release through her clenching muscles.

Her body trembled on the precipice of ecstasy, her muscles tightening around Donovan as waves of pleasure crashed over her. She clung to him desperately as she fought to maintain control.

"Professor," she gasped, her voice thick with need. "I'm so close ... Please, may I cum?"

Donovan shook his head slowly. "Not yet, my sweet girl," he grunted, his voice commanding. "I want to torture you."

He slowed his thrusts, drawing out each movement with agonizing precision. Sienna whimpered, her body aching for release.

"But I need it," she pleaded, her hips rocking against him instinctively. "Please, PLEASE!"

Donovan's lips curved into a wicked smile. "Oh, but you can wait, and you will. I want to see how long you can resist ... how much pleasure you can take before you break."

His cock slid in and out of her with agonizing slowness, the thick ridge of his head dragging against her most sensitive spots with each stroke.

She could feel every vein, every pulse of his shaft as it filled her before withdrawing almost entirely, leaving her aching and empty.

"Please," she whimpered, her voice breaking. "I can't take much more."

Donovan's eyes burned with desire as he watched her struggled. He leaned in close.

"Come for me," he whispered. "I'll let you."

Those words were all it took for Sienna to cry out in pleasure as she climaxed, her juices flowing freely to coat Donovan's shaft.

She clung to him. His fingers dug into the flesh of her hips as he continued to pound into her relentlessly, his eyes locked onto hers with a fiery intensity that promised satisfaction like no other.

"Good fucking girl," he praised.

He continued crushing her pussy, causing her to unleash a torrent of orgasmic release over his pulsing shaft.

As Donovan neared his climax, Sienna broke free and dropped to her knees.

"In my mouth!" she demanded.

Her soft lips wrapped around Donovan's throbbing member, engulfing every inch of his manhood. Her eyes locked onto his, communicating a potent mixture of lust and gratitude that left him pulsing. The sensation of warm, wet suction was overwhelming, sending shockwaves of pleasure radiating out from his loins. Donovan watched Sienna savor every last sensation. His body trembled as he felt the orgasm overtake him completely.

She let out a soft moan as she tasted his hot seed spill into her waiting mouth. She never broke eye contact, savoring the moment and showing Donovan just how obedient she could be.

She held up her tongue to reveal the creamy mess he had made before she swallowed it all down, eager to prove herself as a good little girl. The taste of him on her lips gave her a sense of pride and she relished in the power she had, yet still submitting to his every command.

With a soft whisper, she grinned, "Thank you, Professor," before taking him back into her mouth. She savored the sight of his reaction, watching as his eyebrows furrowed and his lips parted with pleasure. The taste of him lingered on her tongue, a mix of salt and musk.

She maintained a perfectly submissive posture before him, her lips curving into a grin as she gazed up. "There you go, Professor," she purred, satisfaction evident in her tone. "I cleaned you all up." His eyes roamed over her pretty little face, taking in every curve as he spoke.

"You're a sexy little brat, if I may say so."

Sienna's legs trembled as she rose, steadying herself against Donovan's solid frame. The water cascaded over them, washing away the evidence of their passionate encounter. Donovan pulled her close, his arms enveloping her in a tender embrace that contrasted sharply with their frenzied lovemaking.

As he nuzzled her hair, his voice became thick. "You're unbelievable," he whispered.

Sienna nestled into his chest, savoring the warmth of his skin and the steady thrum of his heartbeat. For a moment, she allowed herself to imagine a future where moments like these weren't stolen or hidden. Where their dynamic wasn't confined to secrets and hushed whispers.

But reality intruded as Donovan reluctantly released her, reaching for the shampoo. "We should get cleaned up," he said softly. "Checkout is eleven."

With gentle hands, he lathered her hair, his fingers massaging her scalp in soothing circles. Sienna closed her eyes, committing every sensation to memory.

A bittersweet melancholy settled over them. The reality of their situation began to sink in, the fleeting nature of their encounter becoming all too apparent. Sienna's fingers trembled slightly as she turned off the shower and wrapped a plush hotel towel around her body.

Donovan sensed her unease and pressed a tender kiss to her forehead.

His deep voice rumbled through his chest, "It'll be okay. We'll figure it out."

Sienna nodded. She busied herself with drying off and gathering her clothes from the night before, which were scattered across the hotel room floor. She stole glances at Donovan, admiring the way his muscles flexed as he buttoned up his shirt.

"I should probably head back to my room," Sienna said softly. "I need to pack."

Donovan's eyes softened.

He held Sienna's face in his hands, lifting her chin to meet his eyes. "I wish we could stay together longer," he whispered, softly stroking her cheek with his thumb.

Sienna leaned into his touch, her heart aching. "Me too."

With a soft sigh, Donovan kissed her cheek. "Go pack."

Nodding, Sienna gathered her composure and slipped out of the room. The hallway felt cold and empty after the warmth of Donovan's embrace. She hurried to her own room, her mind swirling with memories of their night together.

As she packed her suitcase, Sienna's mind raced. How could she go back to being just another student in his class after everything they'd shared? The thought made her stomach churn with anxiety.

Donovan's fingers tightened around the handle of his suitcase as he made his way through the hotel lobby. The scent of shampoo still clung to him. His mind raced with conflicting emotions—desire, guilt.

He forced himself to focus on the check-out process, but his mind kept drifting back to Sienna. The softness of her skin, the way she trembled beneath his touch, the breathy moans that escaped her lips.

"Is everything alright, sir?" the receptionist asked, noticing his distraction.

"Yes, fine," Donovan replied gruffly as he signed the final paperwork.

His phone vibrated in his pocket as he approached the valet. Donovan smiled as he saw Sienna's name appear on the screen. He unlocked his phone and read her message.

The image that greeted him caught him off guard. Sienna's creamy thighs were barely covered by delicate pink panties, rhinestones glittering along the straps. The single word accompanying the photo—"Yours"—made his heart beat faster.

"Sir?" the valet interrupted his thoughts. "Your car."

Donovan cleared his throat, trying to regain his composure. "Thank you," he managed.

His hands shook with a mix of anticipation and anxiety as he settled into the driver's seat. He didn't waste any time in responding, typing out a possessive message: "Mine." The weight of that one word overwhelmed him.

Meanwhile, Sienna approached the front desk, her cheeks still flushed from their earlier activities. The clerk smiled warmly at her.

"Checking out, Ms. Holloway? I hope your stay was pleasant."

Sienna nodded; her voice soft. "Yes, thank you. It was ... memorable."

The clerk tapped at her keyboard. "Your father just paid the bill. You're all set."

Sienna's eyebrows shot up. "My father?"

"Yes, an older gentleman. I'm guessing he was your dad. He wanted to make sure everything was taken care of for you."

The noticeable age difference between them suddenly felt more pronounced. Yet instead of being intimidated, Sienna found herself oddly aroused by the thought.

"Oh, yes," she stammered, trying to maintain her composure. "Thank you for reminding me. He ... he mentioned he might do that."

"Jesus," she whispered to herself, biting her lower lip. "What have I done?"

Her fingers fumbled with her phone, nearly dropping it as she read the response to the daring photo she had sent: "Mine."

She quickly typed out a response: "Thank you for ... everything. When can I see you again?"

Her phone buzzed with Donovan's reply: "Class."

Her response was quick and instinctive: "Yes, Professor," a submissive nod to the power he held over her in both the classroom and the bedroom.

As she retrieved her car from the valet, Sienna's mind raced with thoughts of her next encounter with Donovan. The illicit nature of their relationship caused a mix of sensations within her, both thrilling and fearful. The thought of being caught added to the thrill, while also causing a sense of unease.

With a shaky breath, she started the drive back home, which seemed eternal. Her body ached with longing, already missing Donovan's touch.

As she neared her parent's house, reality began to set in. How would she face him in class now? How could she sit there, pretending nothing had changed when everything had?

Distracted

The low drone of Professor Hayes giving another lecture faded into a distant hum as Sienna's gaze drifted to the window, autumn leaves dancing on a bre'eze outside, but her mind was elsewhere—the conference.

"The socioeconomic ramifications of the Industrial Revolution..."

She shifted in her seat, trying to focus on his words. "Can anyone tell me the primary factors that led to urbanization during this period?"

Sienna knew the answer. She always knew the answers in his classes. But now, with the weight of their secret hanging between them, she found herself paralyzed. Her hand twitched, wanting to rise, but she held back.

What if he called on her? What if their eyes met and everyone saw the dynamic between them?

"Ms. Holloway?" Donovan's voice jolted her. "You're usually quite vocal on this topic. Any thoughts?"

Sienna's heart raced. She opened her mouth, but the words wouldn't come. "I ... um..."

"It's alright," Donovan said, his tone gentle. "We'll come back to you."

Sienna sank into her chair, mortified. She'd never faltered like that before. But now, every glance from Donovan felt loaded with hidden meaning. Every casual brush of his hand against the podium reminded her of touches far more intimate.

She tried to pull herself together, scribbling nonsense notes to appear engaged. But her mind kept drifting back to stolen moments and whispered promises.

"Remember," Donovan continued, "context is crucial in understanding historical events."

Sienna wondered—what was the context for what they were doing? Where could this possibly lead? The questions swirled in her mind as Donovan's presence commanded the room.

His voice resonated through the classroom. "Ms. Holloway, how did the Industrial Revolution alter the social and economic dynamics?"

Despite locking eyes with him, Sienna remained oblivious to Professor Hayes calling on her. She blinked rapidly, trying to shake off the fog of distraction. Suddenly, a sharp elbow dug into her ribs.

"Wake up, Sienna!" Her classmate, Lisa, warned her with blue eyes grabbing her attention more than the words being spoken. "He's looking right at you."

Sienna's cheeks burned as she met Donovan's expectant gaze.

"I ... I'm sorry, Professor Hayes," she stammered. "Could you repeat the question?"

Donovan's expression softened, but then turned slightly disappointed.

He moved on and the rest of the lecture passed in a blur of shame.

Students began packing their things and rising from their seats. Donovan's commanding voice reminded them. "Don't forget, the essay assigned last week on the Silk Road is due tonight. Please upload your completed work by eight pm."

Sienna bolted for the library, her sanctuary, skipping her next class. "SHIT! SHIT! SHIT!" she cursed herself as she ran across the campus. She was so engrossed in the weekend with Donovan that she forgot to spend any time on her essay.

She spread her materials across a worn oak table, determined to focus. "Come on, Sienna," she muttered to herself. "You can do this."

The words blurred into meaninglessness. Unbidden images flashed through her mind: Donovan's hands, strong and sure; his lips warm against her skin; the intensity in his eyes as he'd whispered, "Pretty girl."

Sienna shook her head violently, trying to dispel the memories. "Focus," she whispered fiercely. But her body thrummed with remembered pleasure, making concentration impossible.

She traced her finger along a line of text, willing herself to absorb the information. But all she could think about was how those same fingers had trembled under Donovan's touch, how he'd made her feel both powerful and utterly vulnerable.

The ticking of the library clock mocked her efforts. She felt her grip on her academic life slipping further away, consumed by the intoxicating whirlwind of her feelings for Donovan.

"Maybe I should text him," she whispered, pulling out her phone. Her thumb hovered over his name in her contacts. "No, that's stupid. It's only been a day."

She placed the phone on the table, but lifted it up moments later, clearly struggling with a decision. "But what if he's thinking about me, too?"

The internal debate raged, each moment of hesitation costing her precious study time. With a frustrated groan, she shoved the phone into her bag.

"This is ridiculous," Sienna muttered, running her hands through her hair. "I need to finish this."

She turned back to her laptop, forcing herself to type. The words came haltingly, each sentence a struggle against the tide of distraction.

"It doesn't have to be perfect," she told herself, even as guilt gnawed at her. "Just ... done."

The library gradually began to empty. The flickering lights from above cast eerie shadows, intensifying her feeling of being alone. She was completely immersed in her task, or perhaps more accurately, lost in her thoughts about the past weekend. Before she knew it, the entire day had passed, and she had spent it all inside the library.

Finally, with a mix of relief and shame, Sienna hit "Submit" on the online portal. She knew it wasn't her best work, not even close. But it was finished.

"Professor Hayes will know," she whispered, her cheeks burning. "He'll see right through it."

Gathering her things and fleeing the library, the weight of her inadequacy pressed down on her with each step.

Weeks passed, and Sienna's academic performance continued to spiral. Her usual meticulous notes devolved into distracted doodles and half-finished sentences, punctuated by the occasional heart with "D.H." inscribed within.

Sienna's hand no longer shot up to answer questions. Instead, she slouched in her seat, avoiding eye contact and praying not to be called upon. When assignments were returned, her once-perfect scores were replaced by disappointing Cs and Ds.

She drug herself into class one morning with a sense of foreboding. Donovan had a habit of grading work by hand and returning them. But on this specific day, the task of returning the work seemed to take forever. After what felt like hours, he finally reached Sienna's paper: the dreaded Silk Road essay.

The paper crinkled in her trembling hands; her eyes fixed on the glaring red "C-" scrawled across the top. Her stomach twisted as she read Donovan's neat script at the bottom: "See me after class."

The room emptied around her, chairs scraping and voices fading as students filed out. Sienna remained rooted to her seat, heart pounding against her ribcage.

Finally, she approached Donovan's desk, clutching the assignment like a shield. "You ... wanted to see me, Professor Hayes?"

Donovan looked up, his dark eyes searching her face. "Sienna." His voice was low and concerned. "Is everything alright? This isn't your usual work."

She swallowed hard, fighting the urge to fidget. "I'm fine," she mumbled, avoiding his gaze. "Just ... had an off day, I guess."

"An off day?" He repeated, leaning back in his chair. "Sienna, you've consistently been one of my top students. This feels like more than just an off day."

Heat crept up her neck as memories of their night together flooded her mind. She struggled to form a coherent response. "I've been ... distracted. It won't happen again."

Donovan's brow furrowed. "Is there anything you'd like to talk about? Anything ... troubling you?"

Sienna's breath caught. Did he know? Was he hinting at their shared secret? She tugged at the sleeve of her sweater, buying time. "No, nothing specific. Just ... personal stuff. You know how it is."

"I see." His tone was carefully neutral. "Well, if you need any additional support or resources, please don't hesitate to ask. Your success is important to me."

His words hung heavy in the air between them. Sienna nodded quickly, desperate to escape. "Of course. Thank you, Professor. It won't happen again."

As she turned to leave, Donovan called out softly, "Sienna?"

She paused, heart racing.

"Remember, your studies should always come first."

She nodded once more, not trusting herself to speak, and hurried from the room, the weight of his gaze following her every step.

The rest of her classes passed with nothing but disgrace on her mind. She had disappointed Donovan Hayes, and that was not something she could take lightly.

As the sun started to set, she pushed open the doors of the library, their weight feeling more heavy than usual. The familiar scent of old books and dust enveloped her, but tonight it felt suffocating rather than comforting. She made her way to her favorite secluded corner, her footsteps echoing in the near-empty building.

"Focus," she whispered to herself, spreading her notes across the worn wooden table. Her eyes caught on Donovan's handwriting, his red pen slashing through her mediocre work. She traced his words with her fingertip, remembering how those same hands had touched her...

"No." She shook her head violently, copper strands falling loose from her ponytail. "Stop it," she hissed under her breath.

She forced herself to reread the chapter on medieval trade routes, but Donovan's voice resonated in her mind, lecturing on the Silk Road. She could almost smell his sandalwood cologne, feel the heat of his body next to hers.

"This is impossible," she groaned, burying her face in her hands.

But as the hours ticked by, Donovan's presence seemed to permeate every page, every word. His voice echoed in her head, praising her past work and expressing disappointment in her recent failing. The weight of his expectations pressed down on her, mingling with her own desires until she could barely breathe.

Sienna rubbed her eyes, exhaustion settling into her bones.

"Burning the midnight oil, Ms. Holloway?"

Donovan's deep voice jolted her. She looked up, meeting his dark eyes. His presence, so unexpected in the late-night quiet, startled her.

"Professor Hayes," she managed. "I ... yes, just trying to catch up."

He sat across from her. "Admirable dedication. Though I hope you're not neglecting your other responsibilities."

Sienna swallowed hard, hearing the layers in his words. "No, sir. I'm ... prioritizing."

"Good," Donovan smirked, his gaze flickering to her full breasts pressing against her shirt. "Your academic success is crucial, Sienna. It requires your full attention."

She nodded, heart racing. "I understand. I won't let you down again."

His lips quirked in a small smile, warm yet restrained. "Goodnight, Ms. Holloway."

"Oh, and this is for you." He handed her a small envelope with "Private" written in his elegant script.

Sienna exhaled shakily with a meek, "Thank you, sir."

That evening, safely confined in her cramped bedroom, Sienna finally worked up the courage to open the envelope. Her eyes widened as she read the contents: a dinner reservation for two at Saltwater Bistro, an upscale seafood restaurant that night.

"Oh God," she breathed, her heart pounding. "What am I going to wear?"

She flung open her closet door, frantically rifling through her meager wardrobe. Most of her clothes were practical and modest, a holdover from her conservative upbringing. But buried in the back, she found a short, low-cut black dress she'd never had the nerve to wear.

She gently slid the dress over her head, feeling the fabric caress her skin like a lover's touch. She surveyed herself in the mirror, the low neckline daring and alluring. The dress hugged her curves in all the right places, accentuating her full and tempting breasts. She reached for a delicate chain and fastened it around her neck, the dainty diamond pendant nestling perfectly in the valley of her cleavage.

"He's always checking out my tits," she said to herself as she repositioned the pendant. "Definitely a tit man."

She spritzed on the cheap perfume she'd bought online. The scent was cutesy and artificial, but it was all she had. She took a deep breath, steeling herself for what lay ahead.

With one last anxious glance in the mirror, she grabbed her purse and headed out into the night, her heart pounding with a mixture of fear, anticipation, and arousal.

Dinner

H er heels clicked against the polished marble floor as she entered the restaurant, the scent of seared seafood and aromatic herbs enveloping her. Her eyes darted nervously around the dimly lit space, but the absence of Hayes' commanding presence sent disappointment through her chest.

"May I help you, miss?" A hostess approached, her smile polite, but scrutinizing.

Sienna's quiet voice barely carried above the chatter in the room as she spoke. "I have a meeting with someone ... Professor Hayes."

"Of course. He hasn't arrived yet, but I can seat you at your table."

As Sienna followed the hostess, she felt the weight of several gazes upon her. A group of well-dressed businessmen at the bar openly admired her figure, their eyes lingering on the low neckline of her dress. Heat rose to her cheeks, a mixture of embarrassment and unexpected pleasure.

Seated at an intimate corner table, Sienna fidgeted with her necklace, her fingers tracing the delicate chain. The minutes ticked by agonizingly slow. Just as doubt began to creep in, the restaurant's atmosphere shifted.

Donovan's presence immediately commanded the room. Their eyes met across the crowded space. His salt-and-pepper beard framed a subtle smile.

"Good evening, Sienna," he greeted, his deep voice wrapping around her like velvet as he took his seat next to her. "I trust I didn't keep you waiting long."

Sienna's voice trembled as she stuttered out her response, "N-no, sir." The air between them felt charged, the small table forcing their bodies close together. Sienna could feel the heat radiating off Donovan's body. His knee brushed against hers beneath the crisp white tablecloth. She was sandwiched between him and a smooth wooden wall, the feeling of being trapped only added to his dominance.

The scent of his sandalwood cologne mingled with the aroma of fresh herbs. "Please, call me Donovan when we're in public."

She took a deep breath, willing her nerves to settle. "It's a lovely restaurant, Prof—Donovan. Have you been here before?"

His eyes sparkled in the soft candlelight. "A few times. The seafood here is exquisite." He leaned back. "How was your day, Sienna? Did you have any other classes?"

As they fell into conversation, Sienna felt her anxiety slowly melt away. She found herself captivated by Donovan's rich, melodious voice as he described a particularly engaging lecture he'd given earlier that day.

"You seem really into history," Sienna remarked, blushing slightly. "I'm sorry I didn't do so well on my essay."

Donovan's expression grew serious. "Actually, Sienna, that's something I want to discuss with you. That essay was ... concerning."

Sienna's stomach dropped. She'd been dreading this moment. "I-I know, Professor—I mean, Donovan. I'm so sorry. I was distracted, but I promise I'll do better."

Donovan's brow furrowed with genuine concern. "You've always been an excellent student. I'd hate to see our ... connection interfering with your studies."

Sienna's cheeks flushed with embarrassment. "I just ... I can't stop thinking about you."

Donovan leaned in closer, his voice low and husky. "Sienna, look at me."

She raised her eyes to meet his intense gaze. The candlelight flickered across his handsome features.

"I'm flattered," he explained, "and I won't deny that I find you ... captivating." His eyes wandered briefly to the swell of her breasts, barely contained by her dress. "But your education must come first. We need to find a way to channel this energy productively."

Donovan's gaze lingered on her neckline for a moment, tracing the delicate lines of her dress before eventually meeting her eyes.

Their waiter approached, his presence a gentle intrusion on their growing intimacy. Donovan turned to him with an air of authority, his deep voice resonating as he spoke.

"We'll have the filet mignon and the Alaskan king crab legs for two, please. Oh, and a couple of glasses of your house Pino Grigio, please."

A knot of anxiety formed in Sienna's stomach. She'd never eaten crab, nor tasted wine, let alone in such an upscale setting. Her fingers nervously toyed with the diamond pendant at her neck.

Donovan's perceptive gaze caught the slight tension in her shoulders. He leaned in, his cologne—a familiar scent comforting her.

"Is everything alright?" His voice lowered for her ears only. "If you'd prefer something else, I'm sure we can change the order."

Sienna swallowed hard, her cheeks flushing. "No, no, it's fine," she stammered, not wanting to disappoint him. "I'm just ... not used to such fancy meals."

A soft chuckle escaped Donovan's lips. "There's a first time for everything, pretty girl. I'll guide you through it."

"Tell me, Professor," she asked, her usual timidity giving way to a playful tone, "do you often take such an ... interest in your students' culinary education?"

Donovan's eyes sparkled with amusement and something darker, more intense. He leaned in closer.

His words hang heavy in the air, dripping with implication. His gaze lingered on the pendant drawing attention to Sienna's soft cleavage, a twisted smile playing on his face before meeting her eyes again. "Only the most ... promising ones," a hint of hunger in his voice. "And you, Miss Holloway," he paused, savoring her anticipation, "have shown exceptional potential."

Sienna felt her cheeks flush, a mix of embarrassment and arousal coursing through her, making it difficult to maintain composure.

"You're quite fetching when you blush, Miss Holloway." His words, feather-light, tickled her ear.

Sienna blushed even deeper. She ducked her head, her long, flowing hair falling forward like a curtain, obscuring her flushed face. She took a deep breath, trying to regain her composure.

"I hope to live up to your expectations, Professor," she managed.

Donovan grinned. "I have no doubt you will exceed them."

Sienna's heart raced, her fingers trembling slightly as she reached for her wine, which seemed to appear out of thin air.

She felt Donovan's foot slowly trace up her calf. She nearly choked on her wine, setting the glass down with a soft clink.

"Are you alright?" Donovan asked, concern lacing his tone, though his eyes glimmered with mischief.

Sienna nodded, unable to trust her voice. She pressed her thighs together, trying to quell the growing ache between them. She struggled to contain the whirlwind of emotions and sensations threatening to overwhelm her.

Donovan's hand, heavy with heat and desire, traced the curve of her thigh, searing through the thin fabric of her dress. The warmth spread through her like a wildfire, igniting every nerve in her body. She could feel her heart race as he slowly inched his fingers higher, their tips teasing just beneath the hemline.

His fingers brushed the barest edge of her panty line, or rather, the absence of it. His eyebrows arched in silent question, his fingertips touching the delicate lips of her succulent pussy. The sensation spread throughout her entire body as Donovan's skilled fingers explored her most intimate parts. His touch was delicate and light, teasing her slick folds and igniting a tingling sensation that shot through her core.

She reached for her wine glass, quickly drinking its entire contents.

"Whoa, girl!" Donovan tried to slow her down.

Sienna gasped, coughing at the wine burning her throat.

Donovan's touch lingered, teasing her clit for just a few seconds before he withdrew his hand.

Heat suffused her cheeks as she realized her arousal was on display for him, and most everyone else in the restaurant, to see. Unable to meet his gaze, she focused on the long, white tablecloth, hoping it would hide his wandering hands from onlookers. She shifted slightly in her seat, torn between the desire to press closer and the need to maintain some semblance of decorum.

"I see you're as affected by this as I am," Donovan growled softly in her ear.

Sienna turned to him, her emerald eyes dark with desire and lust. "I ... uh-huh," she trailed off, words failing her as she struggled to process the whirlwind of emotions and sensations coursing through her body.

The moment hung suspended, thick with unspoken desire, until a polite cough shattered the tension.

"Your meals, sir, madam," the waiter announced, appearing suddenly at their table.

Sienna jerked back, her face flushing as crimson as her hair. Donovan, ever composed, simply nodded to the waiter, his expression indicating nothing of their intimate exchange even while his strong hands held a firm grasp on her soft, inner thigh hiding under the tablecloth.

"Thank you," he said smoothly, his deep voice steady.

Sienna's eyes focused on the steaming dishes. The aroma of perfectly seared steak and succulent crab filled her nostrils, momentarily distracting her from the lingering heat of their interrupted moment. "This looks delicious."

Donovan's eyes met hers over the rim of his wineglass. "I'm sure it will taste even better," he replied, his tone rich with innuendo.

Sienna focused on devouring her steak. She could feel Donovan's gaze on her, intense and unwavering. With each bite, she struggled to maintain her composure, acutely aware of his presence.

"How is your meal?" Donovan asked, his voice intimate.

Sienna swallowed hard. "It's ... exquisite. I've never had steak quite like this."

"I'm pleased you're enjoying it," he said with concern. "Though I notice you haven't touched your crab yet."

Sienna's cheeks burned as she glanced at the untouched crab on her plate. "I ... I don't know how to crack it open," she admitted, embarrassment coloring her tone.

Donovan's eyes sparkled with amusement. "Allow me to demonstrate," he offered, reaching for her plate.

With practiced ease, he selected a crab leg from her plate. His long, dexterous fingers caressed the shell, tracing its ridges and valleys. Sienna watched, mesmerized, as he expertly cracked the leg.

"Pay attention," he said as his hand moved slowly over her skin. "It's all about finding the perfect places, and you know how skilled I am at that."

Sienna giggled.

He gently pried the shell apart, revealing the succulent white meat within. Sienna's mouth watered at the sight; her earlier nervousness forgotten in the face of Donovan's confident display.

"Now," he continued, his dark eyes locked on hers, "the key is to savor every morsel."

Donovan extracted a perfect bite of crab meat, holding it up to the soft candlelight. Sienna held her breath as he brought the morsel to her lips.

"Open," he commanded softly.

Sienna parted her lips, her heart racing as Donovan gently placed the crab on her tongue. The sweet, briny flavor exploded in her mouth, eliciting a small moan.

Sienna savored the delicate flavor, her eyes fluttering closed. When she opened them again, Donovan was watching her intently, his gaze dark with desire.

He selected another piece of crab, holding it tantalizingly close to Sienna's lips. As she leaned forward, he pulled it away with a playful smirk. Sienna's cheeks flushed, her breath quickening as Donovan teased her, bringing the meat close before withdrawing it again.

"Patience, my dear," he chuckled softly. "Good things come to those who wait."

Finally, he allowed her to take the bite, her tongue darting out to catch a stray drop of butter. Donovan inhaled sharply; his eyes fixed on her mouth.

"You're a quick learner," he praised, his voice low and heated. "Now, why don't you try?"

With trembling hands, Sienna picked up a crab leg. Under Donovan's watchful gaze, she attempted to crack it open, her movements clumsy and hesitant. The shell resisted her efforts, slipping in her grasp.

Donovan gently took her hand in his, showing her the right amount of pressure to apply. With a satisfying crack, the shell broke and revealed the delicate meat inside. She extracted a broken morsel of crab, holding it up with a mixture of pride and nervousness.

"Very good," Donovan praised, his voice a low purr. "Now, feed it to me."

She mimicked Donovan's earlier actions, bringing the crab to his lips. His eyes never left hers as he opened his mouth, accepting the offering.

"I like having things on my tongue," Donovan growled.

"I hope you enjoyed it," her voice breathy.

Donovan leaned in close. "Oh, I most certainly did, and I look forward to savoring more delicacies with you."

The evening drew to a close, and the restaurant's patrons began to filter out. Sienna's heart raced, her body still thrumming with unfulfilled desire as she and Donovan stood to leave.

"I ... I had a wonderful time, Professor Hayes," she said meekly.

Donovan's dark eyes locked onto hers, his gaze intense. "As did I, Miss Holloway."

They moved towards the exit; their bodies close but not quite touching.

"Will you be alright getting home?" Donovan asked, his hand hovering near the small of her back as they stood at her car door.

Sienna nodded. She hoped he would invite her back to his place, but she bit her lip, holding back her eagerness.

"I'll be fine," she finally managed. "Thank you for dinner."

Donovan's eyes roamed over her face, lingering on her lips. "The pleasure was all mine," he said softly.

As they stood at her car, tension between them, Sienna hoped for a kiss as she tilted her chin up slightly.

With a deliberate and calculated movement, Donovan leaned in closer to her. His hand glided down the length of her spine before coming to rest on her curvy buttocks.

"I do hope to see an improvement in your classroom performance. There are consequences for those who fail to meet expectations."

With a firm and possessive grip, he squeezed her butt, pressing his dominance over her body. She could feel the raw strength in his touch, a reminder of his control and power over her. Her skin tingled with both pleasure and fear as she surrendered to his grasp, knowing that he held all the cards in their passionate game of love and lust.

"Yes, sir," Sienna echoed, her voice filled with longing.

"Good girl." Donovan patted her ass gently, planted a kiss on her cheek, and opened her car door. "I'll see you in class."

Sienna giggled and sat in the driver's seat. Donovan closed the door and began walking to his SUV.

It was in that moment, without words, they both knew this was far from over.

Office Visit

Sienna's heart raced as she pushed open the oak door to Professor Hayes' office. His signature scent washed over her, intensifying her nerves.

He glanced up from his desk, surprise flashing in his dark eyes. "Miss Holloway? I wasn't expecting you."

"I'm sorry to interrupt, Professor." She hesitated for a moment before stepping inside and gently closing the door behind her. Her fingers found the lock, twisting it with a soft click.

The air in the small office seemed to thicken, charged with unspoken tension. Sienna's gaze darted around nervously, taking in the towering bookshelves and the late afternoon sunlight filtering through the yellowed blinds.

"Is everything alright?" Donovan asked in his deep and silky voice. He leaned back in his leather chair, regarding her with a mix of concern and curiosity.

Sienna's throat constricted as she swallowed, her mouth suddenly feeling like a desert. Her words stumbled out in a rush, her cheeks flushing with embarrassment.

"I-I just ... needed to see you."

Her mind screamed at her, questioning her actions. But her loins refused to listen, leading her down this path toward the one person who occupied her idle thoughts.

"I see. Well, you have my full attention, Miss Holloway." His intense gaze seemed to pierce right through her.

She took a tentative step closer.

"I can't stop thinking about ... about what happened at the conference and then at dinner," she admitted softly.

He chose his words carefully. "Yes, the events surrounding the conference were completely inappropriate. Dinner, too."

"I'm sorry, but I can't say I regret it."

She nervously tried to gather the courage to ask her next question. "Do you feel the same way?"

"Sienna, this is dangerous territory."

"I understand, but I can't deny how I feel."

"There are many risks involved," Donovan rebutted. "I must be careful to protect my career and reputation."

Her heart sank at his words, but she couldn't bring herself to leave. Instead, she took another step closer, her body betraying her better judgment.

"I know," her voice quivered. "But I can't help it. I crave you."

Donovan's eyes darkened, a flicker of desire passing over his face before he schooled his features. "Miss Holloway," he said. "You shouldn't be here. This is not a good idea."

But even as he spoke, Sienna could see the conflict in his eyes. She summoned every ounce of courage she possessed and closed the distance between them, coming to stand in front of him in his chair. The scent of his cologne enveloped her, making her dizzy with want.

"Please," she breathed, her hand trembling as she reached out to touch his arm. "I can't stop thinking about you. About us."

Donovan's jaw clenched. He spoke her name low and slow.

"Siennaaaa..." He warned, but there was a note of longing in his voice that made her pulse quicken.

Her fingers brushed against the polished desk. Without breaking eye contact, she gently pushed against his chest, causing him to roll backward slightly in his chair.

"Ms. Holloway, what are you—" Donovan's eyes went wide as she sank to her knees, disappearing beneath the desk.

The confined space was filled with the heady scent of sandalwood and tobacco. Her breath came in short, shallow gasps as she positioned herself between his legs. She couldn't stop herself, driven by an irresistible desire.

Donovan inhaled sharply, his chair creaking as she pulled it towards her, closing the gap between her and the prize she sought.

"This is ... You ... You are a good little girl and a very naughty brat," his normally authoritative voice tinged with a forbidden approval.

Her emerald gaze locked onto his eyes. A hint of hesitance lingered in her expression, but it was overshadowed by a bold hunger that radiated from her. Her delicate fingers traced the outline of his growing erection, her touch tentative yet eager.

"Is it ... unwelcome?" she asked softly, her voice confident with desire. The air between them was thick as she kissed up his inner thigh, seeking permission for what she desired most.

A moment of tense silence stretched between them. Donovan's dark eyes smoldered as he gazed down at her, a mix of desire and hesitation evident in his expression. "Sienna," he breathed, "you know we shouldn't."

The protest died on his lips as Sienna reached inside his zipper, her small hand creeping inside his pants, wrapping around the base of his growing shaft. She gazed up at him, her green eyes wide with desire and a hint of nervousness. "Please, Professor, tell me you want this," she whispered, her voice a juicy invitation.

Donovan closed his eyes, his jaw tense. "Goddammit, Sienna … alright. But don't tell anyone." His voice was low and commanding. It was both exhilarating and terrifying at the same time.

Sienna's heart pounded in anticipation as she nodded, acknowledging the permission, pulling his erection from his pants.

"Holy shit, this is happening," Donovan breathed in disbelief.

Sienna grinned. "Uh-huh," she mumbled, exploring him tentatively at first, her tongue darting out to taste him. Salty, musky, and uniquely him. His taste on her tongue only excited her more.

"Pretty girl," he groaned, his hands gripping the armrests of his chair. "God, yes."

Emboldened by praise, she allowed herself to relax into the experience, her nervousness ebbing away as she became lost in the sensations. Donovan's breathing deepened, and his body tensed as she teased him with increasing confidence.

They were lost in their forbidden lust for each other. The only sounds in the office were their harsh breathing and the soft, wet noises of her mouth.

Her tongue swirled and flicked with renewed vigor, her lips tightening around Donovan's shaft. She could taste the salt of his precum, feel the pulse of his desire and savored every inch of Donovan's engorged member, her eyes locked on his every reaction.

With a determined look, she took him deeper into her warm, wet mouth, savoring the salty-sweet taste of him on her tongue. Her nose was buried in his coarse pubic hair, and she relished the musky scent that rose from his loins.

Her sensuous lips glided down his length slowly, teasingly, pausing at strategic points to flick her tongue against the spots she discovered were most sensitive. The rhythmic bobbing of her head and the wet slurping sounds filled the space beneath the desk.

Her lips created a perfect seal around him, and she used subtle pressure to guide him in and out of her warm, welcoming mouth. Meanwhile, her soft fingers manipulated his balls, massaging them gently and then pulling on them just enough to elicit a gasp. She knew that soon, she would be able to savor the fruit of her labor—his hot, salty release— which she eagerly anticipated.

Donovan's breath grew ragged as Sienna's ministrations intensified. His fingers gripped the armrests of his chair so tightly his knuckles turned white. Every nerve ending in his body seemed to be on fire, all sensation focused on the exquisite warmth of Sienna's mouth.

"God DAMN, you little brat," he groaned.

She redoubled her efforts, her tongue swirling around his shaft as she took him deeper. She could feel him throbbing against her lips, pulsing with need.

His hips began to move involuntarily, thrusting gently into her mouth. His breathing became more erratic, punctuated by soft grunts and moans. Sienna reveled in the power she held over him, this distinguished professor reduced to a quivering mess by her touch.

She could feel him swelling. His quiet groans grew louder, more urgent.

"Sienna, I'm close," Donovan warned, his voice strained.

She hummed in acknowledgment. Her emerald eyes locked onto his, filled with desire and determination. She took him deeper, relaxing her throat to accommodate his full length.

Donovan's hips bucked involuntarily. His fingers tangled in Sienna's soft red hair, guiding her movements. The wet, slurping sounds of her eager mouth filled the office, mingling with their heavy breathing.

"Oh God, yes," he moaned. "Just like that."

Sienna's tongue flattened against the underside of his shaft, applying delicious pressure. Her cheeks hollowed as she sucked harder, coaxing him closer to the edge.

"MAINTENANCE!"

A hearty yelp from the other side of the office door, combined with a set of keys entering the lock sent a bolt of panic through them both. Sienna's heart leapt into her throat. Donovan sat up suddenly, his knees squeezing Sienna's head, urging her to stop.

The sound of the college janitor's earbuds filtered into the room as he pushed the door open.

"Evening, Professor Hayes!" He called out cheerfully, the squeak of his cart wheels accompanying his entrance.

Sienna froze for a split second, her mind reeling. She should stop, pull away, hide—but the thrill of forcing Donovan to maintain composure was too tempting to resist. Instead of retreating, she intensified her efforts, her movements becoming more urgent and desperate.

Donovan cleared his throat, trying to keep his voice steady as he spoke to the janitor. "Evening, Carl. Just finishing up some work."

However, Carl didn't react; his music was blasting in his ears too loudly for him to hear.

Sienna could feel the tension in Donovan's body, the slight tremor in his thighs. She knew he was about to burst. She ran her tongue along his length, relishing his muffled gasp.

Donovan's eyes darted anxiously between Sienna and Carl, grateful that the custodian seemed oblivious to what was happening under the desk.

Carl carried on with his tasks of emptying trash cans and sweeping, his movements fluid and precise.

"H-hey Carl, do you think you can skip m-mopping today?"

Donovan struggled to keep his voice steady, trying not to give away the taboo pleasure, but Carl continued working, seemingly unaware of the request.

"C-Carl!" He repeated, his voice growing more insistent. Still, there was no reply.

Sienna tightened her lips around the base of Donovan's shaft. He again squeezed her head with his knees.

"CARL!" Donovan's frustration boiled over and he raised his voice.

"Mmmmmm." Sienna hummed, her lips tight around Donovan's manhood.

"Yes, sir?" Carl finally pulled an earbud from his ear.

Sienna twirled her tongue around Donovan's pulsing member.

"I'M REALLY BUSY, PLEASE JUST SKIP MY OFFICE!"

Sienna's head broke free, and she grabbed Donovan's cock, stroking it up and down as fast as her little hands could manage.

"No problem!" Carl yelled back, his bad hearing getting the best of him.

Donovan squeezed the armrest of his chair tightly, feeling Sienna's busy hands work magic on his magnificent shaft.

As Carl began to retreat towards the door, Donovan grabbed Sienna's head and shoved her mouth onto his cock just as he erupted in a silent explosion of ecstasy.

His body tensed. He managed to remain still, but the overwhelming feeling of Sienna's mouth around his throbbing manhood made him bang on the desk with both fists tightly clenched.

Sienna welcomed each spurt with a lustful grin, her lips wrapped tightly around him as she balanced between milking him dry and savoring every last taste of his sweet essence.

Carl raised his hand. "G'night Professor," he yelled, his earbuds making him unaware of both the volume of his departing words and the ecstasy being experienced only a few feet from his position.

As the door clicked shut, Donovan let out a shaky breath. "HOLY FUCKING SHIT!" He cried out, his tone a mix of warning and ecstasy. "You're playing a dangerous game."

She hummed in response. "Mm-hmm."

As Donovan's breathing began to slow, Sienna carefully tucked his relaxing member back into his pants, zipping them up with confidence. She emerged from beneath the desk, her legs slightly unsteady as she rose to her feet.

She stood before Donovan, her lips pressed together in a tight grin. Her cheeks were flushed, and her ponytail had come loose, red hair framing her face. She met Donovan's gaze, her eyes sparkling with a combination of satisfaction and nervousness.

Donovan leaned back in his chair, his expression a mixture of satiation and disbelief. "Sienna, that was ... You're a goddamn brat, you know that?"

She nodded, unable to speak just yet. The taste of him lingered on her tongue.

Suddenly, in one swift motion, she closed the distance between them and pressed her lips to Donovan's, kissing him with hunger. His startled gasp was muffled by her mouth, but quickly turned into a low moan as their tongues met.

Their kiss deepened, fueled by the adrenaline and the risk they'd shared. Sienna's tongue danced around his, savoring the taste of him mingled with her own sweetness. The saltiness of his release was intoxicating, and she moaned into his mouth, the vibration of her pleasure only spurring them both on.

Their lips parted, both of them gasping for air. She sucked her bottom lip, a hint of his arousal still glistening on her swollen lips.

"My god, Sienna," he breathed, his voice rough with lust. "I ... I've never..."

She silenced him with a finger to his lips. "Shh ... I know. And we don't need to talk about it." She stepped back, straightening her clothes and fixing her ponytail. "It's our little secret."

Donovan slumped in his chair, feeling utterly spent and drained. A mix of emotions coursed through him - surprise at her bold actions, intrigue at her growing confidence, and an attraction for this young cutie he just can't seem to shake.

"Please, stay for a moment," Donovan requested.

Sienna nodded in agreement, her eyes filled with curiosity and concern. He gestured towards a nearby chair, patting the cushion invitingly. "Let's have a conversation."

Sienna lowered herself into the seat, her mind racing with thoughts and uncertainties. She knew about "post-nut clarity" and braced herself for potential heartbreak.

Donovan's voice was steady, breaking the tense silence between them. "We need to spend time together as more than just physical partners," he stated. "If your feelings for me are genuine, then it's only fair that I figure out my own feelings for you."

He gestured with his fingers towards the area below the desk. "Especially if we're going to continue engaging in these types of activities."

Sienna's voice trembled with shyness as she spoke. "I just ... I think you're really hot and the sex we have is like, mind-blowing," Sienna stumbled over her words. "I don't know if it's love, but I can't stop staring at you! And when you walk into class? Oh my God!"

Donovan was becoming weary of the obsession. "Sienna, if all we're doing is sleeping together, then let's be truthful with each other. If there are deeper feelings involved, then we should discuss them. Do you not think so?"

Sienna sat in the chair, unsure of what her response should be.

"I—I guess so," she stammered.

Donovan's expression was filled with concern. Was he just a professor taking advantage of a young, attractive college student for his own desires? Or was there something more complex going on that he refused to acknowledge? And what about Sienna - did she only want animalistic sex, or was she seeking something more meaningful?

"We should plan a weekend getaway, just the two of us. It'll be our little secret," Donovan suggested. "I'll pick you up Friday at Saltwater Bistro."

Sienna's heart fluttered at the thought of spending an entire weekend with Donovan, but she also felt a nervous anticipation of what could happen between them. "Okay," she replied with a sigh, unable to resist his tempting offer.

"Five o'clock," he instructed. "Don't be late. We'll have a long drive ahead of us."

Sienna rose from the chair and made her way to the door. "Yes, Professor," she submissively agreed.

As she left Donovan's office, both were left with a slight sense of unease regarding the weekend ahead. She worried about coming up with a cover story for her parents. Meanwhile, Donovan couldn't shake the idea that he might actually be developing feelings for this pretty little redhead.

Deer

Sienna shifted her weight from foot to foot, her pulse racing as she stood beside her car in the restaurant parking lot. The sun-warmed metal pressed against her back through the thin fabric of her loose t-shirt.

Donovan's luxury SUV pulled into the lot. He emerged - broad shoulders and lean muscle beneath his tailored button-down shirt, salt-and-pepper beard glinting in the late afternoon light.

Color bloomed in her cheeks. "Hi, Prof—Donovan." She reached for her bag on the ground, bending at the waist, making sure Donovan got a view of her curvy behind.

"What did you tell your parents?" he asked as he opened the back of his SUV.

Sienna bit her lip. "I told them I'm attending a study retreat with the History Club," she said, her voice tinged with a mix of guilt and excitement. "They think we're preparing for midterms."

Donovan's eyebrow arched as he lifted her bag into the trunk. "Clever girl," he grinned as he caressed her cheek with his thumb.

Sienna settled into the supple leather seat, her heart racing with a mix of nerves and exhilaration. The engine purred to life, and they pulled out of the parking lot, the seafood restaurant disappearing in the rearview mirror. Sienna snuck glances at Donovan as he navigated the winding road, his chiseled profile bathed in the golden glow of the late afternoon sun.

She drank in the sight of him—the strong line of his jaw, the sensual curve of his lips, the glint of silver at his temples. That salt and pepper beard lent him an air of sophistication, hinting at a man who had lived, loved, and learned.

The three-hour drive felt like a blur, the passing scenery fading into a darkness as the sun set. Sienna's mind raced with anticipation. Where could he possibly be taking her? A luxurious hotel, perhaps, complete with fluffy robes and room service? Or maybe a beach resort, where they could lounge on beaches and sip fruity cocktails? The possibilities seemed endless, and her excitement grew with every mile they covered. She was content to let her imagination run wild as she awaited their destination.

All too soon, the car slowed to a crawl. Sienna's eyes widened as she took in the charming forest setting. "We've arrived," Donovan noted, his voice tired.

A cabin came into view as they rounded a final curve, nestled among towering pines. It was small and rustic yet charming with its weathered wood siding and inviting front porch. Donovan's hand reluctantly left her thigh as he parked.

"Home sweet home for the weekend," he announced.

They gathered their bags, shoulders brushing as they made their way up the narrow path. The cabin was cozy, almost cramped. A kitchenette occupied one wall, a couch dominated the main space, and a door led to a bedroom.

The interior enveloped them in its rustic charm, the scent of pine and aged wood permeating the air. It played perfectly with Donovan's cologne and natural musk. Sienna took in the plush sofa, the flickering fireplace, and the inviting king-sized bed draped in soft, cream-colored linens.

"I hope this cabin meets your expectations. I wanted to find a place where we could unwind and just be together."

Sienna glanced up at him, her emerald eyes locking with his smoldering gaze. "It's perfect, Donovan. It's so pretty!"

They took a warm shower together, seeking solace in each other's company. The steam from the shower surrounded them, enveloping them in a cocoon of intimacy.

Sienna stepped in first, sighing as the warm water cascaded over her curves. Donovan followed, his tall frame dwarfing her petite body in the tight space.

His strong hands glided over her wet skin, exploring every curve and dip of her petite frame. She shivered despite the heat, pressing herself closer to his solid chest.

She tilted her head back, letting the water soak her long red hair. Rivulets ran down her neck and between her breasts. Donovan's eyes followed their path hungrily. He reached for the shampoo, working it into a lather between his palms.

"Allow me," his deep voice reverberating in the enclosed space.

Sienna turned, presenting her back to him. Donovan's strong fingers massaged her scalp, working the shampoo through her tresses. She leaned forward, a soft moan escaping her lips as she pressed her ass against his groin. The scent of lavender filled the air.

His hands wandered lower, caressing her shoulders and back.

"You're exquisite," Donovan groaned, as he grabbed her hips.

Sienna turned and traced the planes of his abdomen, marveling at the taut muscles beneath. She felt almost dizzy with desire, drunk on his masculine scent mingling with the steam. His hand cupped her breast as his thumb grazed her nipple.

"Please," she whimpered, not entirely sure what she was asking for.

Donovan's deep chuckle reverberated through her. "Patience, pretty girl. We have all weekend."

The water began to run cold, the small cabin water heater struggling to keep up with the long shower. With a content sigh, Sienna turned off the faucet and stepped out, relishing the warmth of the steam-filled room and wrapping herself in a plush towel. Donovan emerged, his dark hair damp and curling at the ends.

Sienna smiled at the sight of him using his "old people mouthwash," as she teasingly called it. The minty, antiseptic scent filled the air as he rinsed and spit, his reflection in the mirror making her heart flutter. He caught her watching him and grinned, as if he knew exactly what was going through her mind. In that moment, Sienna realized how much she could learn to cherish these little moments of normality with Donovan.

She slipped into her worn and tattered night shirt. It was an old favorite that she had owned for years, its soft fabric providing comfort and familiarity. Beside her, Donovan changed into his usual nighttime attire of loose boxers and a simple t-shirt. The cool breeze from the open window gently brushed against their skin. The room was dimly lit by a lone bedside lamp, casting a warm glow over their bodies as they settled in for the night.

With a gentle pull, they lifted the heavy covers of the bed and wriggled their way in. The sheets felt like those in a hotel room—smooth against their skin and pleasantly cool to the touch. It was a new experience for them, lying in bed in a romantic setting instead of just for physical pleasure. They intertwined their limbs and snuggled close, searching for the perfect position for optimum comfort. After some shifting and adjusting, they settled on facing away from one another with their bottoms touching, finding a comfortable rhythm of synchronized breaths. In this moment, they were content and at peace, simply enjoying each other's company in the tranquil hush of the room.

"Goodnight, pretty girl," mumbled Donovan as he closed his eyes.

"Goodnight, Professor," whispered Sienna.

Moments passed.

"I love you."

Donovan didn't respond. A light snore indicated he had already fallen asleep.

The soft tunes of birds singing outside the open window roused Sienna from her sleep. The sun had yet to rise, but the sounds of nature were slowly stirring awake. She rose from the bed, padding to Donovan's side to peer out the window and take in the world beyond their cozy room. Donovan grumbled beside her, reaching out to touch the small of her back.

"Good morning, beautiful," Donovan growled.

"Good morning, my love," Sienna replied, trying to elicit a response. Donovan remained silent, leaving her wondering if he heard or ignored her greeting.

She glided across the room towards the bathroom, her soft legs catching the moonlight that streamed through the open window. Deciding to enjoy the quiet morning, she made her way through the kitchenette to the cabin door. Donovan trailed behind her, switching on the coffeemaker that he had set up the night before, then heading back towards the bathroom to freshen up.

The crisp autumn breeze caressed Sienna's face as she stepped out onto the cabin's porch, her oversized shirt enveloping her petite frame. She inhaled deeply, savoring the earthy scent of pine and damp leaves that permeated the air. As her eyes adjusted to the dark pre-dawn landscape, she gasped at the sight before her.

In the meadow, just a stone's throw from the cabin, a small herd of deer grazed peacefully. Their tawny coats glistened with dew, their delicate movements exuding a sense of tranquility that seemed to still the world around them. Sienna stood transfixed, her heart swelling with a childlike wonder at the unexpected beauty of the moment.

Inside the cabin, Donovan had changed into pajama pants and busied himself making the bed, the aroma of freshly brewed coffee wafting through the air.

Sienna's soft footsteps drew Donovan's attention. He turned to find her standing in the doorway, her eyes alight with excitement. "Donovan, c'mere," she breathed, her voice low as to not startle her new friends. "There's DEER!"

"I have something for them," Donovan said, retrieving a storage bag from under the kitchenette sink and handing it to Sienna. In it was an ample supply of deer corn.

Sienna's eyes grew wide with wonder and gratitude, a tear forming at the corner of her eye.

"You're amazing, you know that?" she softly whispered to him.

"Go feed the deer," Donovan instructed with a smile. "Slowly."

Excited, but cautious not to scare off their new company, Sienna tiptoed back to the door. She slowly tossed handfuls of deer corn towards them, watching in awe as they timidly approached and eagerly devoured their treats.

Donovan's heart swelled at the pure joy radiating from Sienna. He joined her on the porch, his arm instinctively wrapping around her waist as they gazed out at the enchanting scene before them. The warmth of Sienna's body pressed against his own, and Donovan marveled at how perfectly she seemed to fit in his embrace.

Sienna's voice, gentle and awestruck, pierced the quiet around them. "It's like a fairytale," she whispered, her gaze fixed on the deer.

Donovan's lips curved into a tender smile as he pressed a gentle kiss to the top of her head. "The world is full of magic, Sienna," he whispered, his voice warm and reassuring. "And I think I'd like to be the one to show it to you."

Sienna slipped back into the cabin. "I'll be right back," she called over her shoulder, her voice filled with a newfound lightness. Donovan sat on the wooden bench on the porch, the wood, damp with morning dew, cold on his back.

Moments later, Sienna emerged with a cup of coffee, the steam warming her face. She settled beside Donovan on the porch, handing him the cup.

"I can be a good wife. I'm not ALWAYS a brat," she teased, her emerald eyes seeking his, a hint of vulnerability in her gaze.

"I have no doubt about that, Sienna," he replied, his voice soft yet assured.

"But we *are* going to have to get you to enjoy a normal cup of coffee," Donovan advised as he tried to hand her the cup.

"Nope," she countered playfully. "You keep your nasty bean juice."

The golden rays of the sunrise danced across their faces, casting a warm glow on them. Sienna's hair, tousled from sleep, shimmered like flames in the morning light, and Donovan found himself enchanted by her natural beauty.

In a moment of quiet contemplation, Sienna turned to face Donovan, her voice trembling with a mixture of nerves and determination. "I can't deny how I feel towards you," she confessed, her fingers tightening around his. "It's like nothing I've ever experienced before."

Donovan's heart raced at her admission. "Sienna," he began, his words careful yet laced with an undercurrent of longing, "I must admit I'm beginning to develop some sort of feelings as well. But we need to be cautious. There's so much at stake."

Sienna nodded, her eyes shining. "I know," she whispered, "But I'd like to explore this ..."

"Courtship," Donovan clarified. "Let's call it a courtship. We'll take it slow," he promised, his dark eyes holding her gaze. "One step at a time. We'll navigate this together."

They dressed for the day and ventured into the charming tourist town nestled in the heart of the wilderness. The quaint streets were lined with boutiques, art galleries, and local craft shops, each one beckoning them to explore.

As they passed by a jewelry store, Donovan gently tugged Sienna toward the entrance. "Let's take a look inside," he suggested.

Sienna followed him, curiosity piqued by the shiny things in the window. The store was a treasure trove of glittering gems and intricate designs, each piece more breathtaking than the last. Donovan led her towards a display of necklaces, his fingers skimming over the various glass cases.

"You know," he began, his voice low and intimate, "a pretty girl needs a collar. Something to show the world to whom they belong."

Sienna's breath hitched, her cheeks flushing at the implication of his words. She watched as Donovan asked to see a necklace adorned with a shimmering birthstone pendant, holding it up for her to admire.

"It's beautiful," she whispered, her fingers grazing the smooth surface of the gem.

Donovan smiled, pleased by her reaction. "It would look stunning on you."

As she was about to respond, something in the corner of the store caught her eye. A case displaying a collection of customizable necklaces, each one featuring a gold chain with examples of different lettering. Sienna gravitated towards it, her heart racing with an idea.

"What about this one?" she asked, pointing to the case.

Donovan followed her gaze, a smirk tugging at the corners of his lips. "Interesting choice. What would you have the lettering say?"

Sienna bit her lip, her mind swirling with possibilities. She looked up at Donovan, her emerald eyes gleaming with a mix of innocence and mischief. "What do you want to call me?" she asked, her voice submissive.

Donovan leaned in closely, his warm breath tickling her ear as he playfully ribbed her. "You can write your name or maybe 'Pretty Girl', but you're definitely a bit of a brat," he teased with a fond tone in his voice.

Sienna's heart fluttered with excitement, her pulse racing at the sound of her new, beloved nickname. She turned to the jeweler with determination in her gaze. "Can you make it say 'Brat,' please? And could you make it in rose gold? Oh my gawd, and with a diamond, too?"

The jeweler's smile widened as he quickly jotted down Sienna's request. "It will take about a week for us to get the necklace in. You can return here then to pick it up."

Donovan let out an amused chuckle as he observed his girlfriend ordering what he deemed a typical teenage accessory. He and the jeweler finalized all the details, including the size of that must-have diamond. Meanwhile, Sienna pranced around the store, her eyes sparkling just like the precious jewels on display.

The weekend unfolded in a haze of stolen moments and intimate conversations. Sienna and Donovan found themselves entwined in each other's arms, their bodies seeking comfort and connection. They shared stories of their pasts, their dreams, and their fears, each revelation bringing them closer together.

Sienna marveled at the depth of their bond. It was more than just physical attraction; it was the beginning of a true relationship.

As they lay in bed that final evening, their limbs tangled beneath the sheets, Sienna traced the contours of Donovan's face, committing every line and curve to memory. She knew that their time together this weekend was but a temporary escape from the realities that awaited them back home. But in those moments, nothing else mattered. It was just the two of them, lost in their own world.

The morning light filtered through the cabin's curtains. Sienna blinked her eyes open, a sleepy smile on her lips as she found herself still wrapped in Donovan's arms. His steady breathing told her that he was still asleep, and she took a moment to study his peaceful features.

She untangled herself from his arms with precision and gently left the bed, tiptoeing towards the kitchenette.

As she brewed the pot of coffee, which Donovan religiously prepared the night before, Sienna's mind wandered to the events of the weekend, a kaleidoscope of memories flashing through her thoughts. The stolen glances, the lingering touches, the whispered confessions—each moment was a precious gem, forever etched in her heart.

The aroma of coffee began to fill the cabin, and Sienna poured two mugs, adding a heavy splash of cream and a diabetes-inducing amount of sugar to hers. She brought them back to the bedroom, placing his cup carefully on the nightstand.

Donovan slowly opened his eyes, a gentle grin taking over his features as he saw Sienna. "Good morning, gorgeous," he said in a husky tone, still half-asleep.

"What's that?" Donovan asked, pointing to the light tan liquid in her coffee cup.

"What?" Sienna quickly replied, worried she had done something wrong.

"In your mug? Is that milk?" Donovan chuckled.

Sienna giggled. "No, it's coffee. It's just brat friendly ... And I STILL don't like it."

"You're adorable, pretty girl," he teased. "We have so much more to explore together."

As the morning stretched on, they reluctantly began to pack their bags, the lighthearted banter between them a stark contrast to the rigidness of when they first met. Each item they tucked away felt like a piece of their shared history, a tangible reminder of the memories they had created together.

"I wish we could stay here forever," Sienna confessed as she zipped up her bag.

Donovan wrapped his arms around her, pulling her close. His chin rested on the top of her head as he spoke softly, his voice filled with empathy. "Yeah, it sure is nice here. Don't worry. We'll be back."

Sienna looked up at him, her emerald eyes shimmering with unshed tears. "Promise?"

"I promise," he vowed.

The sun-dappled road stretched before them as Donovan guided the car through the winding curves, the lush greenery of the surrounding forest a blur of emerald and jade. Beside him, Sienna gazed out the window, her mind still lost in the memories of their weekend.

Donovan glanced over at her, his heart swelling with affection at the sight of her so relaxed and carefree. "Penny for your thoughts?"

She turned to him, her eyes sparkling with mischief. "Just thinking about how lucky I am," her hand reaching out to rest on his thigh. "And how much I'm going to miss waking up next to you every morning."

Donovan captured her hand in his, bringing it to his lips for a gentle kiss. "We'll find a way to make it work," he promised.

"Would you like to stay at my place tonight?" Donovan offered. "I'm not ready to say goodbye just yet."

Sienna's breath escaped her, her mind racing with the implications of his invitation. "Yes," she whispered, her voice trembling with a mix of nervousness and anticipation.

"I'll drop you off at the restaurant so you can get your car and then you can follow me home. Does that work for you?"

Sienna was so enthralled at the offer that she completely forgot her car was still at the Saltwater Bistro.

"Oh, yeah! My car!"

They pulled into the parking lot for Saltwater Bistro, and Sienna leaped out of the SUV, all but running to her own car, starting it. The two took off down the road, Sienna following closely behind Donovan.

His house came into view, a charming two-story home nestled in a peaceful neighborhood. The exterior was painted a warm, inviting color, with a well-manicured lawn and a cobblestone path leading to the front door. Sienna followed him inside, her eyes widening as she took in the tasteful decor and the cozy atmosphere.

He led her to his bedroom, a spacious room with a large, plush bed covered in soft, luxurious bedding. The room was dimly lit, creating an intimate ambiance that made Sienna's heart race with anticipation.

Donovan disappeared into the en-suite bathroom for a moment, returning with a brand-new toothbrush in hand. "I picked this up for you," he said, handing it to her with a gentle smile. "I figured you might be spending the night here at some point, and I wanted to be prepared."

Sienna was touched by his thoughtfulness, her heart swelling with appreciation for the man who seemed to understand her so well. She whispered thanks as she took the toothbrush from his hand, their fingers briefly touching in a fleeting moment before separating.

They settled into bed, the soft glow of the television illuminating their faces as they snuggled together under the covers. Donovan's arm draped around Sienna's shoulders, pulling her close to his side as they watched a movie, their bodies fitting together like two pieces of a puzzle.

As the night wore on, they found themselves lost in each other's touch, their hands exploring the contours of each other's bodies with a tenderness that spoke volumes about their growing connection. They shared soft kisses and whispered conversations, their laughter mingling together in the quiet of the room.

Eventually, the two lovers found themselves settling into their newfound favorite sleeping position—with their butt cheeks touching. It was a reminder of their connection throughout the night, a silent reassurance that they were not alone.

Pancakes

Donovan began to stir, his body following its usual routine. His biorhythms were like clockwork, never deviating from their established pattern. It was a little early for him, but only an hour before his normal 5:00 waking hour.

He reached out instinctively, pulling Sienna's soft, warm body close against his own. Spooning her from behind, he buried his face in her fiery hair, inhaling deeply.

His hands began to explore Sienna's curves, tracing feather-light paths across her silken skin. His fingers danced along the gentle slope of her hip, then ghosted over the dip of her waist.

Sienna let out a contented sigh, still half-asleep. She wiggled her hips playfully, nestling her bottom against Donovan's groin. She could feel him beginning to harden and swell with arousal at the contact. She moaned softly. Pulling away slightly, she reached down between their bodies and slid her hand over his swelling shaft, feeling the heat radiating from it.

Rolling over to face him, she gazed up, her emerald eyes glinting with equal parts tenderness and desire. Her full pink lips curved into a smile. "Mmmm, good morning, Professor," she purred. "Seems like someone's already waking up."

Donovan chuckled, a sensual rumble in his chest. He traced a finger along her delicate jawline. "And how could I not be, with such a breathtaking beauty against me?"

Heat bloomed across Sienna's cheeks at the raw want in his gaze, the unabashed appreciation and hunger. It never failed to thrill her, being the sole focus of this brilliant man's attention and passions.

Sienna excused herself and quietly slipped out of the room, heading to the bathroom. A low groan escaped him.

After a few minutes freshening up, she re-entered the bedroom. Donovan was sprawled across the rumpled sheets, his handsome face etched with pleasure as he stroked himself. He was magnificently aroused, his thick shaft glistening at the tip.

A jolt of molten heat speared through Sienna's core. Moisture pooled between her thighs, her body responding instinctively to the erotic display. She bit her lip, transfixed by the sensual motion of Donovan's hand gliding up and down his impressive length.

"Started without me, I see," she scoffed huskily, shrugging off her nightshirt and shedding her panties to stand bare before him. "Naughty professor."

Donovan's heavy-lidded gaze raked over her, his smile wickedly seductive. He couldn't muster words.

Sienna climbed onto the bed, straddling Donovan's hips. She positioned herself over his rigid cock, rubbing the broad head through her slick folds. They groaned in unison at the delicious friction.

Then, with a roll of her hips, she took him inside in one smooth glide. "Oh God, yes," she grinned, exquisite pleasure unfurling within her as she stretched to accommodate his girth.

Strong hands gripped her waist as Donovan thrust up into her welcoming heat. "Christ, you feel good. So nice and tight for me."

They moved together in a timeless rhythm, their bodies in perfect sync. Sienna rode with rising urgency, taking him deep.

"That's it, you pretty little girl. Take what you need," Donovan panted, his dark eyes wild and fevered.

Raw ecstasy spiraled tighter and tighter as Sienna increased her pace. She felt Donovan swell inside her, his body tensing as he neared the edge. "Come for me," she demanded breathlessly, clenching around him. "Fill me up. Now."

With a guttural shout, "FUCK!" Donovan let go, his release flooding inside her. The sensation triggered Sienna to squeeze and capture every drop of his explosion, gushing inside her like a tsunami.

Finally, Sienna collapsed onto Donovan. Donovan peppered Sienna's face with soft kisses, murmuring endearments. "Good girl ... Thank you."

Sienna patted Donovan's chest affectionately, a satisfied smile playing on her lips. "You did good, Professor," slightly out of breath. "Very, very good."

With a contented sigh, she carefully climbed off him, sticky with his seed dripping from her pussy. Donovan reached for her, knowing this was a quickie, but that she hadn't yet had her orgasm.

Sienna playfully swatted his hands away. "No, thank you, mister. I'm good for now."

She stretched, catlike, the dim light caressing her bare skin. Donovan's eyes roamed over her appreciatively, drinking in every curve and freckle. God, she was breathtaking.

She settled back against the pillows, pulling the sheet up to cover herself. Donovan sat up beside her, his body still humming with residual pleasure. A comfortable silence stretched between them.

Donovan cleared his throat. "Should we, uh, should we be worried? About potential consequences?" He gestured vaguely towards their lower bodies.

Sienna turned to look at him, green eyes soft with understanding. "You mean a baby?"

Donovan nodded, suddenly feeling awkward discussing such a serious topic naked in bed. "I mean, we get carried away at times. I should've used a condom, or..."

"Hey, it's okay," Sienna reassured him, placing a hand on his arm. "I'm on the pill. Have been for a while now. We're okay."

Relief washed over Donovan's face. "Right, of course. I just wanted to make sure we were on the same page."

"We are," Sienna said confidently, lacing their fingers together.

Donovan kissed her knuckles reverently. "Good girl."

Sienna, still not quite ready to leave the realm of slumber, drifted back into a peaceful sleep. She was content giving Donovan his release.

He remained seated against the headrest, reading the news on his phone until his alarm clock started blaring, shattering the moment.

"Wha—huh?" She blinked owlishly, adorably disoriented. Her bleary gaze landed on the clock, and she groaned. "Ugh, why's your alarm going off at the butt-crack of dawn?"

"Because some of us have early morning responsibilities," Donovan teased, bopping her on the nose. "Plus, I like to have a few moments to myself before the world needs me. Not everyone gets to laze about until the cushy hour of 10:00 A. M."

"Hey, I'll have you know morning classes are the bane of my existence," Sienna huffed in mock indignation. "Forgive me for not being an early bird like you, grandpa."

"Grandpa?" Donovan narrowed his eyes at her. "Careful, young lady. This old man might have to teach you some manners."

Sienna smirked up at him through her lashes. "Promise?"

Their playful banter dissolved into laughter and languid kisses, heralding a new day ripe with responsibility.

Donovan's hand skimmed down Sienna's side to rest on the enticing curve of her hip. "I believe it's time for breakfast." He placed a delicate kiss on the tip of her nose. "Can't have you wasting away from hunger, now, can we?"

Sienna let out an exaggerated huff. "Oh, I suppose you're right. Breakfast does sound good." She rolled onto her back and stretched seductively, the covers slipping down to reveal a tantalizing expanse of creamy thigh. "Mmmm, I'm thinking pancakes. With peaches and whipped cream."

"Your wish is my command." Donovan trailed his fingertips across Sienna's collarbone. "I'll make my famous vanilla whiskey sauce to pour over the peaches. Gives them an extra kick of flavor."

Sienna's eyes widened. "Vanilla whiskey sauce? You're just the king of making sauces for my tongue, aren't you?" She poked him playfully in the chest. "Is there anything you can't do, Mr. Tall, Dark, and Multi-Talented?"

"Well, I've yet to master the art of resisting your charms." Donovan captured her hand and pressed a lingering kiss to her palm. "But I'm quite happy being captivated by you."

A delicious shiver raced through Sienna. It amazed her sometimes, the effortless way Donovan could set her body humming with the barest touch or sultry word. She twined her arms around his neck, savoring the warm solidity of him, the spicy-sweet scent of his skin.

She wiggled out of bed, her bare breasts catching Donovan's eyes as they had always done. She slipped on her long, loose nightshirt, foregoing panties. Donovan slipped on some pajama pants and a t-shirt.

Offering his arm to her with exaggerated gallantry, Donovan placed a kiss on her forehead. "Shall we, my love? A culinary adventure awaits."

Sienna giggled and tucked her hand into the crook of his elbow, her eyes sparkling up at him. "Lead the way, my valiant chef." And with that, they set off towards the kitchen.

Lost in admiration of Donovan's firm butt, teasing her through his shorts, she failed to notice the silky white ball of fluff lounging in her path until it was too late. She let out a squeak as she tripped over Baby, Donovan's cat with fluffy white fur and striking blue eyes.

"Whoa there!" Donovan spun around just in time to catch Sienna, strong arms encircling her waist. "You okay?"

"Yeah," Sienna stammered, cheeks flushed with embarrassment. She shot Baby a baleful glare. "Just didn't see the kitty cat speed bump."

Baby regarded them both with an air of regal disdain, as if they were the ones inconveniencing her. Donovan chuckled, bending down to scratch behind her ears. "Don't mind Baby. She likes to make her presence known."

"I've noticed," Sienna grumbled, but her annoyance melted away as she watched Donovan interact with his beloved pet. There was something incredibly endearing about seeing this powerful man go all soft and gooey over a cat.

As if sensing her thoughts, Baby rubbed against Donovan's leg, purring loudly. Then, with a flick of her tail, she sauntered off, apparently having deemed Sienna unworthy of attention.

"I guess I don't get any love," Sienna mused.

"Baby's always been a bit of a diva," Donovan agreed with a fond smile. "But she's been a loyal companion through thick and thin. I don't know what I'd do without her."

The vulnerability in his voice tugged at Sienna's heartstrings. She slipped her arms around him from behind, resting her cheek against his back. "You'll never have to find out. Baby's not going anywhere. And neither am I."

Donovan shifted his body to face her and gently held her face in his hands. "I'm counting on it," he whispered, before pressing a loving kiss on her lips.

They stayed in each other's embrace, enjoying the simple pleasure of being close. After a long moment, Donovan flashed a smile.

"Oh yes, I believe I promised you pancakes. And not just any pancakes—with homemade whipped cream on top."

Sienna's eyes sparkled with anticipation.

"Yes. All the cream. Lead the way, chef."

Donovan moved with the same graceful efficiency in the kitchen that he brought to every aspect of his life. Sienna settled on a stool at the island, content to watch him work his magic.

As he cooked, Donovan regaled her with stories of his culinary adventures, from disastrous childhood attempts to full Thanksgiving spreads. Sienna hung on his every word, captivated by this new side of him.

"I never knew you were so passionate about food," she marveled.

Donovan shrugged. "There's a lot you have yet to learn about me, pretty girl. But we have all the time in the world for that."

"Food is special," Donovan continued. "It's intimate. It's going inside you. It takes trust."

Sienna slipped off the stool and sauntered over to him, hips swaying. Her sleep shirt rode up with each step, offering tantalizing glimpses of bare skin. She pressed herself against his back, nuzzling his neck. "Need any help?" she purred as she squeezed his butt.

"Brat," he growled, his voice rough with desire. "Keep that up and we'll never make it to breakfast."

Sienna giggled, unrepentant. She loved knowing she affected him just as much as he affected her and craved the push and pull of their attraction.

She ran her hands over his chest, feeling the muscles tense beneath her touch. Then, in a bold move, she slipped one hand under the waistband of his pajama pants, teasing his cock.

Donovan hissed, his hips jerking back involuntarily. "Siennaaaa..."

But two could play at this game. In a lightning-fast move, he spun around and lifted her onto the counter, knocking the breath from her lungs. Sienna gasped; her eyes wide as her warm ass slapped upon the frigid granite countertop. He stepped between her parted thighs, hands gripping her hips.

"Naughty girl," he admonished, nipping at her lower lip. "What am I going to do with you?"

"Anything you want," Sienna breathed, wrapping her legs around his waist. She was already aching for him.

Donovan's eyes darkened with lust, his control fraying at the edges. For a moment, Sienna thought he might take her right there on the kitchen counter, pancakes be damned.

But then, with a massive effort, he reined himself in. He ran his fingers quickly up her pussy, teasing her clit for just a second, then licked his fingers clean.

"You, back to your stool," Donovan commanded, pointing to the same stool from which she came, in plain view of where he was working.

Sienna pouted, but obediently hopped off the counter and went to her assigned seat with a submissive "Yes, sir."

"Now," Donovan ordered with fervor in his eyes. "Masturbate while I prepare your breakfast. Show me how my brat plays with herself."

She eagerly reached down between her legs and slowly parted her folds. Her fingers trembled as they lightly traced over her swollen clit, eliciting a groan from deep within her. She teased herself, circling her small nub with just the tip of her finger, building the pressure until she felt her muscles tighten and her breath hitch.

"Goddamn, you're gorgeous. I could watch this all day," Donovan growled.

"FUCK ME GODDAMMIT!" Sienna demanded.

"I'm cooking breakfast," Donovan teased. "Keep going."

She pressed two fingers deep into her pussy, curling them up and massaging her G-spot. Her hips bucked against the stool, grinding against her own hand in a primitive rhythm. She could feel the pressure building inside her, the familiar coil of pleasure winding tighter and tighter.

Her breathing grew heavier, and her body trembled with anticipation. She could feel herself getting wetter, the slickness between her legs a testament to her arousal.

Donovan watched her intently, his hands working efficiently on the stove, but his mind fixated on Sienna. He licked his lips as he watched Sienna's fingers dance between her legs, her moans echoing in the kitchen.

"You're going to make me cum watching you cook, aren't you?" she panted, tilting her head back.

Donovan smirked. "I sure as fuck hope so," he growled, reaching into a drawer and pulling out a small bottle of vanilla bean paste. "Come for me, you fucking brat. Breakfast is almost ready, and you can't eat until you cum."

"Yes, sir," she obeyed.

Her hips bucked against the cold stool, grinding against her own hand in a desperate search for release. Her breaths came in short, ragged gasps as she neared the brink of orgasm.

"Fuck," she moaned, arching her back and throwing her head back. "I'm gonna come for you, Professor. Only for you. Watch me."

Donovan watched intently as Sienna's body shook with pleasure. His cock strained against his pajama bottoms. He pushed her a little further.

"That's right," he growled. "Be a good girl. Let me see."

She spread her legs wider on the stool, exposing herself even more as her orgasm built to its peak. Her fingers worked faster and harder against her clit, rubbing it with just the right amount of pressure to send her over the edge.

"FUCK!" she screamed as her whole body convulsed with pleasure. Her fingers pressed deep into her soaking wet pussy, digging into the flesh around her G-spot as she came hard against her own hand as wave after wave of pleasure radiated through her.

Donovan smiled smugly as he watched his bratty student cum all over herself. He closed his eyes for a moment, savoring the feeling of power that coursed through him when he saw Sienna at her most vulnerable and exposed. When he opened them again, he saw that Sienna was holding on to the table for dear life, panting heavily but looking satisfied for the moment.

"Very nice. Now, clean up the mess you made on that stool," Donovan instructed in a parenting tone. "Hurry. I'm hungry."

She wet a paper towel at the sink and cleaned the stool, aiming her bare ass at Donovan while she wiped.

"Did I do a good job, sir?"

"Well done," he said with a grin. "Now wash up and get ready for breakfast like a good girl."

He slid a stack of fluffy golden pancakes onto a plate, then turned his attention to the toppings: peaches, simmered in vanilla whiskey and butter until they were soft and fragrant. Pillowy clouds of freshly whipped cream, lightly sweetened with hints of vanilla bean speckled throughout.

Donovan finished plating their breakfast with artistic flair. A dusting of powdered sugar, a sprig of mint for garnish. It looked like something straight out of a gourmet magazine.

"This smells amazing," Sienna gushed as he set a plate in front of her. "You're spoiling me."

"That's the idea," Donovan winked, pouring them each a cup of coffee—black for him, a tiny splash of cream for her.

Sienna's eyes glared at the sight of the steaming cup of coffee placed in front of her.

"Is that for me?" she asked in disbelief, pointing at the mug.

Donovan gave a small smile. "Of course," he answered, his deep voice laced with amusement. "It's actual coffee."

A look of disgust crossed Sienna's face as she grabbed a bag of sugar from the pantry. "GROSS!" she cried, quickly dumping an obscene amount into her mug, stirring vigorously. "You and your nasty bean water."

Donovan laughed heartily. "What creamer should I pick up for you?" He asked.

"Name-brand caramel macchiato and Italian sweet cream," Sienna quickly recited. "I like to mix them."

"Of course. Why didn't I think of that?" chuckled Donovan. "I'll have them for you tomorrow."

Sienna was taken aback slightly. Tomorrow? Was she coming back here again tonight? What would her parents think?

Thinking quickly, Sienna spoke up. "N-no rush. I need to focus on my studies this week. Maybe I can stay again after we pick up my collar."

"A wise decision," Donovan agreed. "We tend to get preoccupied when we're together."

They both smiled at each other and tried to focus on the breakfast in front of them.

Sienna savored the last bite of her pancakes, licking a dab of whipped cream from her lips with a contented sigh. Donovan watched her, his eyes darkening with desire at the innocent yet sultry gesture.

"You missed a spot," he grinned as he leaned in to capture her mouth in a slow, deep kiss. He tasted like a heady combination of coffee and maple syrup.

When they finally parted, both slightly breathless, Sienna rested her forehead against his. "I don't want this morning to end," she whispered, trailing her fingers along the stubbled edge of his jaw. "Being here with you, like this ... it feels like a dream."

"It's not a dream, pretty girl." Donovan pressed a tender kiss to her palm. "And as much as I wish we could stay, we both have responsibilities that need tending."

Sienna pouted, but she knew he was right. Donovan had classes to teach, and she had her own coursework to focus on.

"I'm going to miss you like crazy until I see you again."

Donovan grinned. "What do you say we start planning our next date? I was thinking we can head up Saturday morning to pick up your new collar..."

Sienna shivered. The collar would mark her as his.

"Yes, Professor," she breathed, delighting in the way his pupils flared at the title. "I can't wait to wear your collar, to belong to you."

"My pretty girl, my little brat," Donovan praised, catching her lips in one more scorching kiss before reluctantly pulling away. "Now go get that cute butt dressed before I drag you back to bed and traumatize my poor cat."

She moved through the bedroom with a dancer's grace, her slender form backlit by the golden morning light spilling through the windows. As she gathered her clothes from the night before, she snuck glances at Donovan's naked body as he started getting ready for the day.

Her gaze lingered on the hard planes of his chest. Even in repose, he took her breath away and made her ache with a desire that went beyond the physical.

Donovan's eyes turned to her, a slow, sensual smile curving his lips. "See something you like, pretty girl?"

Sienna blushed, caught out, but couldn't suppress an answering grin. "Always, Professor. You're the most beautiful thing I've ever seen."

Donovan's smile softened, his eyes glowing with affection. "Funny, I was just thinking the same thing about you."

As she slipped on her panties and clasped her bra, a sudden thought occurred to her.

"Hey, Donovan? What should I do with the toothbrush you gave me last night?"

"Hmm?" He blinked, momentarily distracted by the sight of her perky breasts nearly spilling out of the lace cups. "Oh, there's a drawer cleared out for you in the bathroom vanity. And feel free to leave anything else you might need. I'm happy to share my space with you."

Sienna froze, one leg halfway in her jeans, stunned by the magnitude of his offer. Leaving personal items at his place, staking a claim in his space ... it was a huge step, a sign of his commitment to a shared future. To her.

Tears stung her eyes as a wave of overwhelming emotion crashed over her. "Really? You ... you want me to keep things here?"

Donovan's brow furrowed as he crossed the room to her. Cupping her face in his big hands, he brushed the tears from her cheeks with gentle thumbs.

"Yeah, I think I'll keep you around," Donovan assured her.

"Keep me?" Sienna's mind was racing, reading into his words.

"Focus," Donovan's voice snapping her back to reality. "We both have classes to attend. Hell, you have my class first thing. We gotta go!"

The two of them scrambled to get dressed, their eyes constantly drawn to each other. Donovan darted into the bathroom, quickly brushing his teeth and spritzing on his signature cologne.

Sienna's gaze fell upon the bottle, filled with that intoxicating scent that always captivated her. The sweet aroma of tobacco mixed with hints of musk and spice. She instinctively grabbed the bottle and sprayed some on herself. She wanted to carry a piece of him with her all day long. Having his seed inside her from earlier was not enough. She craved his essence, wanting to be consumed by it.

As Donovan tucked in his shirt, Sienna stood there inhaling deeply, relishing in the scent that was now hers. It was a reminder of their intimate connection and a promise of more to come.

Sienna hurriedly exited the door, needing to get back home to gather her class materials. The thought of being part of a typical couple caught up in the daily hustle and bustle, made her smile.

She glanced back at the house, catching a glimpse of Donovan's silhouette in the window. Even from a distance, she could feel the magnetic pull of his presence, the undeniable chemistry that simmered between them.

Alarm Code

Sienna's heart raced as she threw open the door to Donovan's office.

"LET'S GOOOO!"

"Hello, pretty girl." Donovan chuckled at the excitement in Sienna's eyes.

"Come on," he instructed as he completed shutting down his computer and walked with Sienna to his car.

He started his SUV as the two got in. Jazz played over the speakers softly.

"Ewww," Sienna grimaced. "It's like we're in an elevator."

"Quiet, you," Donovan teased.

He opened the moonroof, drawing Sienna's attention to the late afternoon sky.

"I didn't know you had a roof window thingy!" Sienna exclaimed.

Donovan laughed. "It's called a moonroof," he explained.

"What's the difference between a moonroof and a sunroof?" Sienna asked. "Does the name change if it's night or day?"

Donovan smiled at her innocence. "I'm not sure it works like that," he replied, unsure of the nuances himself.

Donovan interrupted Sienna's admiration of the view outside. "I thought we would stay at my place tonight and leave in the morning. Is that alright with you?"

Sienna's face lit up. "Absolutely! But can we get some food? I'm kinda hungry."

"Of course," He agreed. "What does my pretty girl want for dinner?"

Suddenly, a colorful billboard caught her eye. It advertised a popular fast-food chain's latest kids' meal, complete with a toy from her favorite animated movie. Sienna's face lit up with childlike wonder.

"Oh, Donovan!" she exclaimed, pointing at the sign. "Can we get that? Please?"

Donovan's eyebrows raised in amusement. "A kids' meal? Really, Sienna?"

She nodded eagerly, her eyes sparkling. "Please? I love those little toys. And the fries are so good!"

He chuckled, shaking his head. "Alright, alright. Who am I to deny you such simple pleasures?"

As they pulled into the drive-thru, Sienna bounced in her seat, her excitement beaming from her smile. Donovan placed their order, adding a more substantial meal for himself.

"Thank you," Sienna said softly, leaning over to plant a quick kiss on his cheek.

The smell of greasy fast food filled the car as they made their way back to Donovan's house. Sienna couldn't wait to dig in, but she knew better than to start eating in his pristine vehicle.

He pulled into his driveway and parked, the clunk of the gear jolting Sienna from her gazes.

"Okie dokie, my dear," Donovan announced, tapping his hand on Sienna's knee.

Together, they walked through the door and Donovan punched in a code on the security panel.

"If you ever need it," he said, directing his words towards Sienna, "it's zero-five-zero-one."

Sienna's eyes widened in surprise. 'Did he just give me the alarm code? What does that mean?' Her mind raced with thoughts of potential meanings and unspoken implications of his action.

They settled on the couch, Sienna cross-legged with her kids' meal spread before her on the coffee table. She immediately went for the toy, tearing open the plastic wrapper with childlike glee.

Donovan watched her with amusement. A fond smile adorned him as he unwrapped his burger. "So, what treasure did you unearth from that plastic prison?"

Sienna held up a small figurine, her eyes sparkling. "It's the princess! Look, she even has a tiny crown." She turned the toy in her hands, admiring every detail.

"A fitting companion for my own little princess," his voice low and affectionate.

Sienna blushed, ducking her head to hide her smile. She popped a fry into her mouth, savoring the salty taste. "So, what's the plan for tomorrow?"

"I'd like to head out early and beat the traffic," Donovan explained. "Plus, it will give us enough time to pick up your collar. Go ahead and unpack some of your things once you're done with your kid's meal," Donovan instructed with a gentle tilt of his head towards the bedroom door. "Remember, you have an entire drawer and some closet space just waiting to be filled."

"Um, I didn't pack anything to leave here just yet. I only brought what I need for the weekend." Sienna felt slightly unappreciative, but Donovan's demeanor was one of understanding.

"It's okay. Whenever you're ready. No rush."

Sienna nodded, feeling relief and gratitude. She finished her meal, carefully placing the princess figurine on the coffee table before gathering the wrappers.

"I'll just go freshen up a bit," she said, rising from the couch.

"Of course," Donovan replied, his eyes following her as she made her way to the en suite bathroom.

Once inside, Sienna leaned against the closed door, taking a deep breath. She caught her reflection in the mirror—cheeks flushed; eyes bright with excitement. The reality of their weekend getaway was finally sinking in. She splashed some cool water on her face, trying to calm her nerves.

When she emerged again, Donovan was beginning his nighttime routine. She watched as he peeled off his day clothes and replaced them with pajamas. The sight of his bare chest made her head spin with desire.

Donovan caught her stare.

"Is everything alright?" He asked.

"Y-yes," Sienna stammered. "I just love the sight of you."

Donovan approached her with sensitive eyes as he reached to caress her face.

"I love the sight of you as well," Donovan smirked. "You've been on my mind all day today. Let me see you."

She unbuttoned her blouse, revealing inch by inch of creamy skin. The fabric slipped from her shoulders, pooling at her feet. Sienna stood before Donovan in her bra, her chest rising and falling with quickened breaths.

Sienna's fingers moved to the button of her jeans. She hesitated, her eyes locked with Donovan's intense gaze.

"Go on," he encouraged softly.

With deliberate slowness, Sienna undid the button and eased down the zipper. She hooked her thumbs into the waistband, then paused.

"You know," she said, "I could use some help."

Donovan's eyebrow arched. "Is that so?" He took a step closer, the heat from his body enveloping her. "And what kind of help did you have in mind?"

Sienna bit her lower lip, suppressing a grin. "Well, these jeans are awfully tight. I might need some ... assistance... getting them off."

Donovan's hands came to rest on her hips, his thumbs grazing her exposed skin. "What do I get in return for my assistance?"

Sienna leaned in, her lips brushing against Donovan's ear as she whispered, "Whatever you want."

A low growl rumbled in Donovan's chest. His hands slid down to cup her backside, pulling her flush against him. "Be careful what you offer, little one."

With deft movements, Donovan peeled Sienna's jeans down her legs, his fingers trailing along her smooth skin. Sienna stepped out of the denim, now clad only in her matching underwear.

Donovan took a step back, his eyes roaming over her body appreciatively.

"Lay down," He commanded.

"Yes, Professor."

"You are so fucking beautiful," he whispered as he crawled over her and kissed her lips gently. His hands roamed over her body, cupping her breasts and pinching her nipples hard through the fabric of her bra.

Sienna moaned softly into his mouth as she reached down to rub her pussy through the thin material of her underwear. She could feel herself getting wetter by the second at the thought of what was about to happen. Donovan broke the kiss, trailing gentle kisses along her jawline before nibbling on her earlobe.

"Are you ready for me?" He asked, his voice rough with desire.

"Yes," Sienna whimpered, unable to meet his eyes as she waited for him to take control. Donovan kissed down her neck, chest and stomach, drinking in every inch of her porcelain skin. He grasped both sides of her thong and slowly pulled it down, revealing her wet pussy to him. He ran his tongue along the seam of her pussy lips before pushing inside.

Sienna gasped as his tongue delved between her folds, sending jolts of pleasure through her body. His strong hands gripped her thighs, holding her steady as he explored every inch of her most intimate area.

"Oh god," she moaned, her fingers tangling in his salt-and-pepper hair. The scratch of his beard tickled her sensitive skin.

He alternated between long, languid licks and quick flicks of his tongue against her clit. Sienna's legs trembled as the pressure built steadily. She'd never felt anything like this before - so intense, so overwhelming.

Moaning softly, she arched her back in response to the exquisite pleasure coursing through her body. She couldn't believe how good it felt to have him pleasuring her.

Her head fell back as she let out a low moan, reveling in the intense pleasure coursing through her body. "Taste me, Professor. Make me your dirty little secret."

Donovan chuckled darkly, pleased by the way she responded to his advances. His rough hands gripped her hips tightly, holding her still as he continued to lap at her pussy like a starving man at a feast. With one hand, he reached up to pinch a hardened nipple through the lacy fabric of her bra, eliciting a sharp intake of breath from Sienna.

"Tasty girl," he growled against her skin.

Sienna nodded frantically, unable to form coherent words as she was consumed by the sensations washing over her. Her pussy clenched around Donovan's invading tongue, her juices oozing from her swollen clit.

"That's it, my little brat. Let me taste your pleasure."

His words were the final push that sent Sienna tumbling over the edge of ecstasy. She cried out in pure pleasure as waves of sensation crashed over her body, sending her into a state of euphoria. Her legs trembled and quaked as she squeezed them tightly around Donovan's head, holding him in place as he continued to lap at her with gentle, relentless strokes. Her whole being was consumed by the intense pleasure, and she rode it out until every last bit of tension left her body.

Sienna could taste herself on Donovan's lips as he slithered up her body and kissed her deeply. Her body still trembled from the intensity of her orgasm, but she felt a renewed surge of desire as his hard cock pressed against her stomach.

"Was that what you wanted?" Donovan murmured against her ear, his voice low and husky.

"Yes," Sienna breathed. "God, yes. But I want more."

His hands roamed over her body, igniting sparks of pleasure wherever they touched. Sienna moaned as he kissed his way down her neck and across her collarbone before taking one of her nipples into his mouth through the fabric of her bra.

"Please," Sienna begged.

Donovan chuckled against her breast, sending vibrations straight to Sienna's core. "Patience, Brat," he teased. "We have all weekend."

Sienna's fists pounded against the soft, plush mattress in a fit of frustration. "But ... But... Professor! UGGGHHH!"

"I gotta leave you wanting more," Donovan explained. "Besides, it's time for bed. That alarm goes off at your favorite 5:00 hour."

"Gross!" Sienna grumbled.

Sienna pouted, her lips forming an exaggerated frown as she flopped back onto the bed. The sudden shift from intense arousal to disappointment left her feeling restless and unsatisfied. She watched as Donovan moved about the room, his muscular form still tantalizing even in the dim light.

"You're cruel," she hissed, though there was no real heat behind her words.

Donovan chuckled. "Cruel would be leaving you alone all night," he said, sliding into bed, spooning her. "I'm simply ... building anticipation."

His arm snaked around her waist, pulling her flush against his chest as he slid into bed. Sienna could feel the hard planes of his body, the heat of his skin seeping into hers. She wiggled her hips, feeling his half-hard cock press against her backside.

"Tease," Donovan growled in her ear, his hand splaying possessively across her stomach.

Sienna giggled, feeling a mixture of nervousness and excitement bubble up inside her. "Takes one to know one, Professor."

"Go to sleep, Donovan ordered."

Sienna sighed, nestling back against Donovan's warm chest. The steady rhythm of his breathing began to lull her, and she felt her eyelids growing heavy.

"Goodnight, Professor." Sienna's voice was thick with approaching sleep.

"Goodnight, little brat," Donovan replied, pressing a soft kiss to the nape of her neck.

Rose Gold

The shrill beeping of the alarm clock pierced through the peaceful silence of the bedroom, jolting Sienna from her deep slumber. She groaned, burying her face deeper into the pillow as Donovan stirred beside her.

"Rise and shine, little one," Donovan's voice was annoyingly chipper for such an ungodly hour.

Sienna responded with a muffled whine, pulling the covers over her head. "Five more minutes," she pleaded, her voice thick with sleep.

Donovan chuckled, gently tugging the blanket away from her face. "Come now, Sienna. We have a long drive ahead of us."

She cracked open one eye, glaring at him with all the ferocity she could muster at five am. "The sun's not even up yet," she grumbled, her lower lip jutting out in a pout.

"That's the point," Donovan replied, running his fingers through her tangled red hair. "We'll beat the traffic this way."

Sienna sat up reluctantly, her oversized sleep shirt sliding off one shoulder. She rubbed her eyes, blinking owlishly at Donovan.

"Fine," she mumbled, her voice still rough with sleep. "But I demand my sugary coffee. Lots of it."

Donovan chuckled at Sienna's demand, his eyes crinkling with amusement. "As you wish, my little sugar addict. Now, let's get moving."

After a quick shower that did little to fully wake her, Sienna emerged from the bathroom wrapped in a fluffy towel, her damp hair leaving water droplets on her shoulders. Her eyes widened in shock when she saw Donovan, fully dressed and ready to go. His car was already packed, and the bed was made flawlessly.

"Coffee awaits!" Announced Donovan.

Sienna dressed, fumbling with the buttons of her blouse, her fingers still clumsy from sleep. She caught a whiff of Donovan's cologne, which awakened her senses more effectively than the shower had.

"Don't forget your jacket," Donovan reminded her, his voice a warm rumble in the quiet room. "It might be chilly on the road."

Sienna nodded, grabbing her favorite denim jacket and shrugging it on. She glanced at her reflection in the mirror, noting the slight shadows under her eyes and the way her damp hair curled around her face. With a resigned sigh, she quickly pulled her hair into a ponytail and followed Donovan out the door.

Her eyes widened with delight as they stepped into Enchanted Brew. The coffee shop was a whimsical wonderland, with floating candles suspended from the ceiling and shelves lined with curious bottles filled with colorful liquids. The air was thick with the aroma of freshly ground coffee beans and warm spices, making Sienna's mouth water in anticipation.

Her fingers danced across the screen of her phone, her eyes widening with each swipe through the Enchanted Brew's digital menu. The app was a kaleidoscope of vibrant colors and whimsical animations, mirroring the magical atmosphere of the physical shop. As she scrolled, tiny animated coffee beans bounced merrily across the screen, leaving trails of glittering fairy dust in their wake.

She approached the counter, where a barista dressed in a flowing robe and pointed hat greeted her with a smile. "What potion can I brew for you today, my dear?"

Sienna giggled, fully embracing the magical atmosphere. "I'd like a Grande Glitterberry Dream Frappuccino, please! But can you make it with half whole milk and half oat milk, blend in one pump of vanilla syrup, one pump of raspberry syrup, and half a pump of dragon fruit syrup, add a splash of cold brew concentrate for a tiny caffeine kick, layer the drink with blueberry puree on the bottom and a swirl of blackberry sauce in the middle, top it with whipped cream, but can you sprinkle edible glitter and holographic sugar crystals on top, drizzle a mix of white chocolate and strawberry syrup over the whipped cream? Oh, and can you serve it in a clear cup with rainbow sprinkles around the rim?"

Donovan raised an eyebrow but said nothing, ordering a simple black coffee for himself.

As they settled in to enjoy their drinks, it dawned on Sienna. "I left my plushie at home. Can we make a quick stop to grab it?"

"I suppose," Donovan digressed. "Won't your parents wonder why I'm with you?"

Sienna bit her lip, a worried crease forming between her brows. "You're right," she said softly, her excitement deflating slightly. "I didn't think of that. Maybe we shouldn't..."

"It's okay." Donovan saw the discontentment in Sienna's eyes. "We'll make it quick. Let's get going."

They set off on the road to retrieve the forgotten plushie. Sienna burst out of the SUV as they pulled into the driveway.

"BE RIGHT BACK!" she exclaimed as she ran inside.

Donovan watched as the door opened moments later, but instead of Sienna running back, he was greeted by her parents.

Donovan tensed as Mr. and Mrs. Holloway emerged from the house, their expressions a mix of surprise and suspicion. He quickly composed himself, putting on his most professional demeanor as he stepped out of the SUV.

He cleared his throat, his mind racing to formulate a plausible explanation. "Good morning, Mr. and Mrs. Holloway. I apologize for the early disturbance. Sienna forgot some materials for a ... special research project we're working on. I offered to give her a ride to retrieve them before we head to the college library."

Mrs. Holloway's eyes narrowed slightly. "A research project? On a Saturday?"

"Yes," Donovan replied smoothly. "Sienna has shown exceptional promise, and I'm mentoring her personally."

Sienna reappeared in the doorway, clutching a worn, stuffed rainbow horse to her chest. Her eyes widened in panic as she took in the scene before her.

"Mom, Dad," she stammered. "I..."

"Sweetheart," Mrs. Holloway began, her voice laced with concern, "why didn't you tell us about this research project? And why do you have Sherbert?"

Sienna's cheeks flushed as she hugged her stuffed horse. "I ... I didn't want to bother you with the details. It's just some extra credit work."

Mr. Holloway's eyes narrowed as he looked between Sienna and Donovan. "This seems very odd."

Donovan stepped forward; his posture relaxed but authoritative. "My apologies, Mr. Holloway. The library has limited weekend hours, and we want to make the most of our research time. I assure you, Sienna's academic growth is my utmost priority."

Sienna, sensing the tension, quickly moved towards the SUV. "We should get going," she said, her voice higher than usual.

As they climbed into the vehicle, Sienna clutched Sherbert tightly to her chest, her heart racing. She could feel her parents' eyes on them as Donovan backed out of the driveway.

Her parents turned to walk back into the house.

"They better not be sleeping together," Mr. Holloway grumbled to his wife. "I'll kill him."

Once they were a safe distance away, Sienna let out a shaky breath. "That was close," she whispered, her knuckles white as she gripped the stuffed horse.

"Yeah, but we got through it," Donovan sighed. "Let's enjoy the drive up, shall we?"

As far as the eye could see, the countryside stretched out like a magnificent tapestry, rich in hues of emerald and gold. The fields glistened under the warm rays of sunlight, creating a picturesque view. The gentle breeze carried the sweet scent of freshly cut grass, adding to the ethereal feeling of being surrounded by nature's beauty.

As they rounded a bend in the highway, a garish neon sign caught Sienna's eye. "Love Shack Adult Emporium," she read aloud, her cheeks flushing.

Donovan glanced at her, a mischievous glint in his dark eyes. "Care to explore, darling?"

Sienna's heart raced. "I ... I've never been in a place like that," she admitted softly.

"There's a first time for everything," Donovan said, already pulling into the gravel lot.

The shop's interior was a sensory overload. Sienna's eyes darted nervously from shelf to shelf, taking in the array of unfamiliar objects.

Donovan's hand found the small of her back, steadying her. "See anything interesting?"

Sienna pointed to a sleek, curved object. "What's that?"

"Ah," Donovan said, his voice taking on a familiar educational tone. "That's a prostate massager. It's designed for—"

"Oh!" Sienna interrupted, her face burning.

Donovan chuckled, leading her to another display. "Perhaps something more suited to your anatomy?" He held up a small, tapered butt plug.

"Would you like to try it?" Donovan asked in a persuasive tone.

Sienna bit her lip, curiosity warring with apprehension. "I ... maybe? Do they have one in rose gold? I see some with rhinestones. I need it to match my collar!"

With determined brows, she combed through the crowded display, searching for the perfect piece. Her gaze finally landed on a glimmering gemstone that caught her attention.

"That's it!" She exclaimed, pointing to a thin, delicate plug adorned with a sparkling jewel.

Donovan's warm smile spread as he carefully picked up her new treasure. "We'll take our time with it," he assured her, understanding her apprehension.

As they left the shop, Sienna's mind raced with possibilities. The drive to the cabin passed in a blur of anticipation.

Finally, they pulled up to the familiar rustic structure. Donovan carried their bags inside while Sienna looked around for her deer friends.

"I love this place," Donovan said, wrapping his arms around her from behind.

Sienna leaned into him. "I can't wait to make some new memories here."

The two had arrived early enough in the day that they decided to see if the rose gold necklace was ready for pickup.

Memories flooded Sienna's mind with each passing landmark as the two drove into town.

"Good afternoon," a well-dressed jeweler greeted them. "How may I assist you today?"

Donovan cleared his throat. "We're here to pick up a custom piece. Under the name Hayes."

The jeweler's eyes lit up with recognition. "Ah, yes. I remember this one. One moment, please."

As he disappeared into the back room, Sienna turned to Donovan, her cheeks flushed. "It's ready?"

"Patience, pretty girl."

The jeweler returned, carrying a velvet box. With practiced grace, he opened it, revealing a delicate rose gold necklace.

Her collar.

Sienna's eyes went wide as she saw the word "Brat" spelled out in elegant script, adorned with a single, sparkling diamond.

"It's ... it's beautiful," she whispered, her fingers hovering just above the metal, afraid to touch it.

Donovan's eyes never left her face, drinking in every nuance of her reaction. "Do you like it?"

She nodded, unable to form words. The collar represented so much more than just jewelry—it was a symbol of their connection, of the trust and power dynamic they shared.

"May I?" the jeweler asked, reaching for the collar in an attempt to put it on Sienna.

"Not just yet," Donovan interjected smoothly, his tone playful, but firm. "We'll take it as is, thank you."

Sienna's eyes widened, a mixture of desire and frustration flooding her system. "But—"

"This is something I, not anyone else, place on you." The small, velvet box nestled safely in Donovan's pocket brought a sense of nervous excitement to Sienna.

The rest of the day passed in a whirlwind of activity, but Sienna's mind kept drifting back to the velvet box nestled in Donovan's pocket. As they strolled down the quaint main street, her fingers often strayed to her bare neck, imagining the shape of the script against her skin.

They browsed through a series of charming boutiques, each offering a unique treasure. In a vintage bookshop, Donovan's eyes lit up as he found a rare first edition.

As the afternoon sun began to dip, they found themselves in a quaint dog boutique. Sienna cooed over the tiny sweaters and bejeweled collars; her mind once again drawn to her own collar waiting for her.

"Shall we head back to the cabin?" Donovan suggested playfully.

Her voice was filled with anticipation as she practically begged, "Yes, I really want my collar."

As they drove back to the cabin, Sienna's fingers fidgeted in her lap, her mind racing with anticipation. The weight of the velvet box in Donovan's pocket seemed to fill the car, an unspoken promise hanging in the air between them.

The cabin door clicked shut behind them, sealing Sienna and Donovan in their private sanctuary. The air felt electric, charged with desire and tension. Sienna's heart raced as she watched Donovan move deliberately across the room, his presence commanding even in the intimate space.

"Sienna." Donovan's voice was a low rumble. "Come here."

She obeyed instinctively, her feet carrying her before her mind could process the request. As she approached, Donovan reached into his pocket, withdrawing the small velvet box that had occupied her thoughts since leaving the jewelry store.

"Do you know what this means?" he asked, his dark eyes boring into hers.

Sienna swallowed hard. "It means ... I belong to you."

A smile immediately formed at the corners of Donovan's lips. "That's right," he confirmed, opening the box to reveal the rose gold collar. "And are you ready for that responsibility?"

Sienna's mind whirled. Was she ready? The weight of the moment pressed down on her, exhilarating and terrifying in equal measure. "I ... I think so," she stammered, her usual social awkwardness amplified by the intensity of the situation.

Donovan's free hand came up to cup her cheek, his touch gentle yet firm. "You think so? Or you know so?"

His words ignited something within her, a spark of certainty amidst the chaos of her emotions. "I know so," she breathed, leaning into his touch. "I want to be yours."

Donovan's smile widened, pride and desire evident in his expression. He removed the collar from its box, the delicate chain glinting in the soft cabin light. Sienna held her breath as he brought it towards her neck.

"Close your eyes," he instructed softly.

Sienna complied, her heart pounding hard. The cool metal startled her. She felt Donovan's fingers working at the clasp, his breath warm against her ear.

"There," he whispered proudly, his lips brushing her earlobe. "Perfect."

Sienna's eyes fluttered open, meeting Donovan's intense gaze. Her hand instinctively went to her throat, fingers tracing the smooth metal, and the raised letters spelling out 'Brat'.

"Mine," he commanded.

"Yours," she obeyed.

"How does it feel?" Donovan asked, turning her to face the mirror.

"It feels..." Sienna paused, searching for the right words. "Like I'm finally where I belong."

Donovan's response was a low growl as he pulled her close. "Good girl."

Sienna melted into him, all her usual nervousness and social awkwardness dissolving in the heat of their embrace.

As they broke apart, Sienna whispered, "What now, Professor?"

"Now, my pretty girl," Donovan's voice was dark and almost ominous. "We will begin something most important. Dinner!"

Sienna blinked in surprise, her mind still reeling from the intensity of the moment. "Dinner?" she repeated, a mixture of confusion and amusement in her voice.

Donovan chuckled, his eyes twinkling with mischief. "Can't have you fainting from hunger now, can we? We skipped lunch, and it's rather late."

"And here I thought you were going to ravish me right here and now, Professor."

"Patience, pretty girl," Donovan admonished playfully.

They made their way to the cabin's small kitchenette, where Donovan began pulling microwave meals from the fridge. Sienna sat, watching him work. Her fingers kept drifting to her collar, tracing the letters absentmindedly.

Donovan's eyes darkened with desire as he watched her fingers caress the rose gold. "It suits you perfectly," he said, his voice low and husky.

The microwave beeped, breaking the moment. Donovan turned to retrieve their meals, but Sienna could feel the tension simmering between them. As they ate, the conversation was punctuated by heated glances and lingering touches.

As the last bites of their microwaved dinners disappeared, they settled onto the couch, snuggled under a cozy blanket. After scrolling through endless options on their streaming service, they finally settled on a romantic comedy. Sienna rested her head on Donovan's lap.

His fingers idly stroked her hair, occasionally brushing against the nape of her neck where the clasp of the collar rested. Each touch heightened Sienna's senses, igniting a slow burn of desire in her core.

She kept playing with the necklace, thinking about the magnitude of its meaning and the beautiful man beside her.

"Are you even watching the movie, little one?" Donovan's amused voice rumbled through his chest.

Sienna tilted her head up to look at him, her cheeks flushing. "I'm trying," she admitted sheepishly. "But I keep getting ... distracted."

Donovan's eyes darkened. "Oh? And what's distracting you?"

Sienna bit her lip as she moved her hand to hold his half-erect cock. "This."

"Naughty girl. Is that what you want?"

Sienna nodded, her heart racing. "Please," she whispered.

"Shall we retire to the bedroom?"

"Yes, Professor," she breathed.

Donovan stood, taking her hand in his, leading her to the bedroom and turning off the TV.

His eyes glimmered with mischief and desire. "Now, my little brat, we will see just how well you can follow instructions."

He reached out to undo the top button on her blouse. His fingers were shaking slightly, betraying his own excitement as he slowly eased the fabric apart, revealing more of her creamy skin.

"You're so fucking beautiful," he sighed.

Sienna swallowed hard, her pussy clenching at the sound of his voice in her ear. She wanted him to touch her, to fill the ache that was growing inside her with his hard cock. But instead, she obediently helped with the buttons so he could pull off her blouse completely.

"Strip for me," he said firmly, his tone leaving no room for disobedience.

"Yes, sir," Sienna replied, relishing the feeling of being under his control.

"You will address me as 'Professor,'" Donovan directed, his dominant nature asserting itself. "And you will be my brat. Is that understood?"

"Yes, Professor," his brat replied, as she paused to fully digest the thought of being his property.

"Go on, strip," Donovan ordered, his gaze fixated on her every move.

Sienna obeyed, slowly unhooking and removing her bra to reveal her firm breasts with their erect nipples. She unbuttoned her pants and turned around. Donovan watched as her curvy backside emerged slowly. A small wet spot had already formed on her panties from her arousal.

"You've made a bit of a mess," Donovan commented as Sienna turned back around. "Lick it off."

Her breath quickened as she shimmied out of her panties, slowly bringing them to her mouth and tasting herself.

"Mmmmm," she relished, knowing how much it pleased him. She seductively removed them from her mouth and twirled them around her finger. "Do you want some?"

"Bring them here," he commanded.

Sienna walked towards him with the damp fabric still held to her lips. Donovan gently, but firmly, pulled the panties away from her lips and brought them to his nose. He inhaled deeply, savoring her scent.

"Delicious," he groaned, his voice rough with desire.

Sienna's fingers hovered over Donovan's belt buckle, her eyes flicking up to meet his gaze. She bit her lower lip, a silent question in her expression as she traced the leather with feather-light touches. Her breath came in short, shallow pants, her chest rising and falling with anticipation.

Donovan watched her intently. He remained still, letting the tension build between them like an electric current. Sienna's fingers trembled slightly as she tugged on the buckle.

Donovan gave a slight nod, granting Sienna permission to continue. She undid the button of his slacks and slowly lowered the zipper, the sound piercing the silence.

She hooked her thumbs into the waistband of Donovan's pants, gently tugging them down. She sank to her knees as she guided the fabric past his hips, revealing his muscular thighs, her mouth watering at the sight of the bulge in his pants.

Looking up at him through her lashes, Sienna placed a soft kiss on Donovan's hip bone. She felt him shudder under her touch, spurring her on. Her hands glided up his legs, savoring the feeling of coarse hair against her palms. She nuzzled against his inner thigh, inhaling deeply, intoxicated by his masculine scent.

With reverent care, Sienna eased his boxers down, freeing his erect cock. It sprang forth, proud and eager.

Without warning, he stood Sienna up and pushed her face-down onto the bed. She gasped in surprise and arousal as Donovan's hands gripped her hips, pulling her ass up and spreading her legs wide, shoving his mouth right up to her pussy.

"Stay just like that," he ordered. "Don't move."

Sienna trembled as she felt Donovan's breath hot against her exposed pussy. She fought the urge to push back against him, remembering his command to stay still.

A swipe of his tongue along her slit made her whimper in pleasure. Donovan growled, but it wasn't her pussy he was after.

He walked to the nightstand and grabbed the discreet paper bag from the adult store. Its fluorescent lettering beckoned to Sienna, promising excitement and pleasure.

"Keep your beautiful ass high in the air while I prepare your new toy," He demanded.

"Yes, Professor," Sienna's response was breathless with anticipation.

"Good brat," Donovan praised her as he opened the box containing the shiny rose-gold butt plug.

"See how pretty it is?" He asked as he held it up for her to admire.

The metal gleamed under the light, its smooth surface reflecting their desire back at them.

"Your new toy matches your collar perfectly," Donovan sizzled.

"Yes, Professor," Sienna grinned. "Thank you, Professor."

Donovan's erection was just inches from Sienna's lips. She leaned in to take him into her mouth.

"Not yet, you brat," Donovan scolded. "You need to ask permission, and right now is all about training you." He went back behind Sienna, admiring his submissive brat, eagerly awaiting him.

Donovan's hands tightly squeezed her ass, gently massaging the supple flesh as he leaned down to kiss and nip at it. He parted her ass cheeks ever so slightly, displaying her asshole before him.

"This ass belongs to ME!" Donovan aggressively commanded as he landed a firm slap on her ass cheeks. He carefully twisted open the bottle of lubricant, squeezing the bottle over her ass, watching intently as the drops dribbled down onto Sienna's sweet, tight, virgin asshole.

She gasped as the icy liquid dripped from her beckoning asshole, tracing a path down to her pulsing pussy. Her skin prickled with anticipation as the coolness spread over her heated parts, heightening every nerve ending.

He pressed the cold metal plug against her waiting hole. He twisted it slowly, coating every inch with slick lube. Anticipation ran through Sienna's body as she waited for him to claim her.

"Please," Sienna begged, then corrected herself quickly. "I mean, thank you, Professor."

Donovan placed the tip of the plug against Sienna's perfect hole.

"Take a deep breath," he advised, his voice low and husky. "I'll push in as you exhale."

Sienna obeyed, taking a deep breath, holding it for just a second before beginning to exhale.

A grin took over Donovan's face. "Here you go," he snarled as he prepared to penetrate Sienna's asshole for the first time.

"OPEN THIS FUCKING DOOR!"

A muffled voice followed by three pounds on the door jolted the two from their training session. They froze, eyes wide with shock and uncertainty.

"Who could that be?" Sienna whispered, her heart racing for an entirely different reason now.

Donovan frowned, his dark eyes narrowing. "I don't know. Nobody knows we're here."

"OPEN THIS DOOR BEFORE I BREAK IT IN!"

Another muffled scream and another three pounds on the door, more insistent this time.

"Stay here," Donovan instructed. He slipped on a pair of comfortable shorts and moved towards the door.

Sienna rolled over and clutched the sheets to her chest, her mind racing. Who could possibly be at their door? And at this hour?

"Stay here," Donovan commanded. "I don't know what's going on."

Sienna obeyed, but something didn't seem right.

"GPS! Donovan! It's the GPS!" Sienna remembered the GPS tracker her family had demanded she have on her phone.

Her frantic screams were too late. The door was already open.

Her heart froze as she saw the shadowy figure standing in the doorway. A chill ran through her veins as she recognized who it was.

Her Father, Mr. Holloway.